The
Chinese
Contract

The
Chinese
Contract

Avoiding Political Hassles

MARY RANIERI

authorHOUSE®

AuthorHouse™ LLC
1663 Liberty Drive
Bloomington, IN 47403
www.authorhouse.com
Phone: 1-800-839-8640

Published by AuthorHouse   02/10/2014

ISBN: 978-1-4918-6362-6 (sc)
ISBN: 978-1-4918-6361-9 (e)

Library of Congress Control Number: 2014902866

Chapter 1

A PAN-AMERICAN PILOT took off from the Tokyo landing strip and sped across China's Yellow Sea to a Peking landing strip. He listened for the high pitched hui jaw sao which meant he could take the left-hand space. The pilot zoomed down with a screeching nose-dive. Allie clutched the seat arms as the asphalt landing strip rushed up at them. Pain lanced her ears. She let go to clasp her hands over both recent ear-surgeries. If only she could survive the harsh landing and face this Mao Zedong regime! Could she and Barney have made a wise choice in coming to this communist state? America's Chiang Kai-shek had been pushed south to Hong Kong in a hasty retreat.

The plane landed with a jolting bounce, groaning from overstretched metal, then taxied at race car speed toward the airport terminal. Eager to dump his human cargo, the pilot drummed his short western nails while idling for a take off. The freedom of the skies had no smell of fear and suspicion. Not only the pilot, but Allie and her husband, Barney, were gwai-lo, (foreign devils), real and present danger, the bourgeois.!

Barney J. Smith would be firing a welding torch, building a plant, just like the contract read. However, the peasant mind was now in control of the country. It showed in the cabin, reeking of garlic, in air-chocked nicotine, and sewage from restrooms. Would this fare well with his international team mates?

In the crowded cabin, robust women looked identical wearing dusty blue Mandarin jackets. They unsnapped seatbelts and collected gray canvas bags. Their bags differed only by Pinyin name tags. They were feminine counterparts of the masculine Red Guards sitting on the side benches and stationed at strategic points. Their crow black hair differed only between queues or wind blown cuts with forehead bangs. How opposite to the feminine pompadours, caftans, and western suits of the Japanese Allie had seen only yesterday in Tokyo! The Japanese were gracious, always bowing, and more her height. Their tresses made a sharp contrast to Allie's pale amber with a gray streak across the front lobe. "It's too early for a widow's peak at 34," her sister, Sandy had remarked at the last birthday party. She would have related more kindly to the Japanese were it not for the nightmares evoked by her father's stories of their sneak attack on Pearl Harbor.

Yesterday hung in her mind like the popular song. On Phoenix Air, the sleek metal plane as silvery as the Wizard of Oz' tin man, had landed as smoothly as a dove at Tokyo airport. Then the sleek,

2

black limousine had slowed to a halt at the luxurious stop-over. Nothing finer, nor more spacious, than the O'kura Hotel with its fountains, palm and Ming trees, its Japanese gardens. Already, it seemed like years ago. And now, no thanks to the rough landing here in Peking, she could become stone deaf according to Doctor Maddox, her audiologist. With his long white coat flapping open, he had dangled a stethoscope and warned of possible complications. "Your stapes has been replaced with a piano wire to relay sound. Be careful of air flights and bathing . . . don't forget your ear plugs."

Inherited nerve disorder was his diagnosis. She smiled inwardly, thinking of an old jingle . . . Except the culprit-donor was healthy and wise, but not wealthy, her traveling-salesman father!. His pale blue Scotch-Irish eyes crinkled shut when he laughed or joked, incessantly turning up his squeaky hearing aid. Its battery was so large it threatened to break the seams of his shirt pocket. From Nova Scotia he had wended his way across the U.S. continent to court a Louisiana curly-locks. Then the border state of Texas pointed its big thumb West. New Mexico was ripe for the conceiving of both daughters, barely two years apart, Sandy in Phoenix, Allie in Carlsbad . . . Allie shook away the image of a travel weary father, inheriting not only his hearing loss but the tendency to travel, though not for pleasure or job-changing. She recalled her adviser, Miss Evans' remark. "Traveling a year abroad is the same as a year

3

of college . . . good as gold . . . catch the gold ring while you can! Let Barney build his Urea plant, and you build on to your sociology minor, your language skills . . . and how about your painting hobby?"

"And how about my passport to danger!" she retorted with a shiver.

The dye had already been cast. She would take a sabbatical year after spending eight years teaching high school history and several summers tutoring migrant farm workers. This summer, instead of migratory children, the refugees of the Vietnamese boat survivors had already traded places with them, as well as capturing her heart. They were camping on floor mats in vacated military quarters of Oklahoma's Claremore College. Barney would commute from Tulsa's in-service training.

Finally, after a long grueling year, Barney waved the contract, dancing a jig, eager to sign on the blank line below bold lettering: Engineering, Chemical Plant, Tsangchow, PRC. She'd looked up the location and paraphrased: "Busy part of the northeast near the Upper Yangtse, not far from China's most productive coal mine." Inwardly, she'd felt reluctant to become a test-pilot or a daring tight-rope acrobat for a new industry testing its ilk. This could become a dangerous mission for testing cultural spare-offs! Barney recalled her paraphrase and seemed to read her mind, holding up his useless pen to delay the signing, thinking what a long lonely year it would be without Allie! He needed her support and nearness as incorporated in the marital contract. Her hesitation was a challenge, so he kept prompting her with, "Where is your spirit of adventure? "Or, "Think how excited your history class would be with your adventure stories!" And another prompt, "Just maybe some poor Chinese wetback would need your counseling after swimming the Rio Grande."

His inane joking finally won her over She latched onto "the trip would excite her history class, and help her deal with emigrant problems."

The Rio Grande had become a gateway for desperate immigrants. Americans inadvertently helped Mexican wetbacks remain on U.S. soil once settled in over many years. She knew of tender-hearted Border Patrol oversights, cold cases, they considered too heartless for prosecution.

The Upper Yangtze was not the Rio Grande, nor was the peaceful Gulf Coast comparable to the turbulent Pacific Ocean to be crossed. She considered China's open invitation to travel East more of an initiation, a dare-devil taking the gauntlet. Carefully considering the boost to their economy, her response was tongue-in-cheek. "Maybe we can improve Uncle Sam's reputation and earn some mullah, eh Barney?" She tossed her Cashmere sweater over the living room Rattan chair, one of four, purchased at a fire sale.

"Yeah, *stateside* mullah doesn't compare." He yawned, stretching his muscular torso, then jingling his coin pocket winking a brown come hither eye before a second thought . . . "oh yeah, the site representative, Mueller, our ground-work guy; he sets up shop . . . Luke and Leora will be a month ahead of us pulling the ropes. Later on we'll meet operators without wives from France, Great Britain, and Hungary. Three-month contractors. All of us *paper tigers* are leaving our cages."

"Unless we get eaten by Khubla Khan!" She chuckled, recalling the puppets at Sandy's drama school who were programmed to slay gwai-lo. We'll need a safe haven on Ming Ching Day, their Easter. That's the day they sweep off ancestor graves, including the Boxer ghosts of 1900! History says the U.S. Infantry came to the rescue, but that was seventy-five years ago. Dramatics aside, she leveled her eyes, "Maybe we *can* survive by eating *their* rice and praying to Azna, our *Mother God*."

"Or locate a dilapidated Buddhist temple for a safe hideout."

"No, they've been made into businesses, according to Silas H. L. Wu: read your company's printout. Wu left Boston to go back to his village for a visit, then wrote his pamphlet on cooperative changes, both good and bad. Very interesting!"

"Our Urea Plant will be needed with only twenty percent of their fertilizer being chemical. We could help do away with the pigsty outhouses straddled by Mr. and Mrs."

She grimaced as she turned to the book shelf retrieving Funk & Wagnall's New Encyclopedia and quoted statistics: "390 inhabitants per square mile of the eastern heartland; it sounds like standing room only, a Gone with the Wind sellout. Chung-hua means Earth's center, the most populous country in the world and probably the noisiest with everyone chattering in a different dialect."

The manly-looking women in the aisle ahead of her and behind her, assembling their small sacks and tote bags could be part of this crowded population. Allie noticed their straight black hair, almond eyes, and faces as round and yellow as pumpkins. Droopy lids of enchanted characters, but not sleeping beauties! They'd shovel a lot of ashes from coal stoves they had to cook on, but Cinderella's feet would not fit in their canvas shoes with crepe soles, flat heels and round toes. Glass slippers, on the other hand, would be numbing for the pumpkin shell wives with no Prince Charming to keep them very well. Natural abstinence for population control: wife here, husband there, ne'er the two shall meet.

She powdered her turned-up nose in the dinky compact mirror, asking herself, what is the typical face of the ugly American? Her intuition answered back. Be patient, they'll surface sooner or later. She snapped the compact shut on her habit of self lecturing, switching to a silent prayer. Father and Mother God, stay near, remove the fear. But she continued studiously staring at fellow travelers, in fact, some eyes resembled blue sparks from Barney's welding rod, as he soldered with maniac speed. She had often felt blest with the eyes of an experienced artist, memorizing features and expressions for future reference. The oriental were statues when it came to keeping inscrutable stone faces, their earth brown eyes revealing no emotion, but ideograms on thought waves?

The stand-off ended, as Barney nudged her into the main aisle, having waited for most of the passengers to descend the ramp.

They toted their maximum-weight suitcases to the airport terminal, leaving Barney's home-made trunk on the loading dock for the liaison to authorize its transport to the southern part of Hopei Province . . . to Tsangchow.

Packing had been volumes with enough clothing, hobbies, toiletries, and medicals to last the contract year. She tried to leave empty space for purchases from their a so-called *Friendship Store*. The packing of medical supplies had succeeded umpteen inoculations against every possible disease in the book The home-made trunk resembled an early-day wooden coffin Barney constructed for duty-free household goods. He'd ignored the teasing of fellow trainees who asked if he were taking his Chinese coffin with him. Allie kept thinking back to an old Chinese textbook about ancestor worship and reverence for the elderly, the coffin being the best gift they could give their parents. But free duty for household goods was a big loophole. Or Japanese-sneaky?

Who would know the time or necessity of an overseas purchase, taking home artifacts labeled "household." She prayed to use good logic. In fact, she had vowed with a Unity Church group to perform a daily prayer ritual for good conduct, for safety coming and going, for accepting and being accepted, fulfilling a contract, as legally as possible.

Upon entering the Peking airport, they looked around for helping hands, only to meet the butt of a rifle. A Red Guard pushed the shaking pair into a dark corner, his gun pointing the way. Not only was their corner dark, but so was the whole airport. Barney turned red with anger, "Electricity shortage! The damn liaison is late*! What a charade!"*

It wasn't too soon for another prayer ritual. "Well, they're packing the gunpowder they invented, but why don't they recognize my finger puppetry? I keep pointing to the private plane on the ramp. They can see it from the foyer. You can't miss the big lettering on the side: KISSINGER I know we're trying to dodge politicians, but can our industry manage without them?"

"You bet it can!" His tension lessened as he hunkered down on a suitcase next to Allie to weather the stand-off. Still looking livid with fright, they whispered encouragements to each other. Allie tried joking, cupping her hands prayerfully, short finger nails lightly polished. "You . . . me . . . bad dragons maybe wearing white masks . . . inscrutable . . . embarrassment end soon . . ." She got the idea of white masks from the sight of several pedestrians wearing surgical masks and no wonder, with smoke stacks puffing out lethal fumes and everyone holding a small Mexican cigarette. She wished she had a real mask!

Rescue arrived within the hour. A flushed-faced pigmy dressed in black except for a white turtle neck t-shirt toting a packet of official papers. He bowed apologetically, offering his hand, (usually a no-no.)

"Welcome to Peking. My name, Li . . . liaison for Me-ester Jordan, now in Russia. I escort you Hotel Peking; your trunk arrive tomorrow's train. I am maybe what you call on R&R, but Russia, forbidden land! Me-ester Jordan maybe not return."

Gripping their overnight bags, they followed Li to the French Renault with a restless driver. He motioned them to hurry inside, shifting noisy gears and glaring from side to side.

Once settled with hands gripping the side loops for a fast drive, Allie grabbed the chance to quiz Li, "Where did you learn to speak English?"

"I study in states: LA. My uncle in Hong Kong." He shifted sideways to converse from the so-called coffin-corner seat. Barney asked about acupuncture, to which Li spread one hand and pointed with the other to a spot between the thumb and forefinger, <u>ah charades at last</u>, "This is for headache if you prick here. You can purchase take-home kit. You will reside near hospital named for much loved Canadian . . . Bethune."

She smiled, wondering about sore-ear acupuncture, remembering with a sigh when she had perfect hearing. She'd even relished the loud applause, after dancing on a third-grade stage in a Chinese crepe paper costume. Accordion-folding lanterns had dangled overhead: oriental magic with gongs and drums accompanying her wavering ribbon. Dallas schools loved pageantry, using China as a land of intrigue, <u>Fu Manchu</u>, <u>Lost Horizon</u>, <u>Hunza</u>, rolled into one. "Made in China" appeared on every toy once Allie turned it over to study its construction. She wondered if all inventions came from Peter Pan's China, the never-never-land. Now the magic had been opened like a lotus bud, but the militia denying its beauty tainted its color with their own military drab. The seeds could take root again she thought, shaking her shoulders to expel childhood dreams, forcing her mind to the advisor's gold ring, and to her new dream of upgrading America's reputation of removing *ugly* from the popular phrase of the ugly American. After all, imports labeled "made in China" had brought about their contract for building a plant. She inwardly chuckled to recall her sister's bonanza. A label that read only "China" proved a boon when her spinster sister, came upon a collection of rare figurines at a California beachfront. Sandy's instinct for antiques and labels thereon led to the must-have artifact. Its label went back to pre-trading days prior to any American imports, a one-time owner closing out an estate. This was Sandy's bonanza! Allie's bonanza would be the good dragon of co-existence, getting along with her international family and coming to an understanding of the leap forward where everything appeared to be abnormal, pointless, restricting . . .

"What is the exchange rate of dollar-for-Yuan?"

Li's chortle accompanied a thumbs up. Screeching of bicycle tires and honking horns made conversation hopeless and gave Allie more ear-ringing. At least she understood the thumbs up to be a positive sign for the exchange rate. The wheels and riders were cloned machinations, the riders garbed in identical blue reflecting ultramarine from bicycle steel frames. Some bicycles waved animal-shaped balloons advertising their commune, and oddly, they too, reflected their color-spectrum of oversize tunics and baggy-pant-garb, all held hostage by the last rays of a spectral sunset. The wheels were not likely from Hong Kong's industrial district, but from the made-in-China People's Republic, blue steel, sporting red stars. Lan se, Hong se, blue and red.

Rearing up from bicycle seats, their faces were taut with fear. Large, dark pupils peered into the small black Renault, reminding her of Pearl Buck's Good Earth . . . wasn't this the year of the dragon? She had opened a going-away gift, E-Ching sticks! After throwing the sticks, she'd read from the manual. Bao zhong, take care, when walking on fire-dragon stones. How to apply the sticks to her dream: after a long day packing Samonite bags, she'd dreamed of an international circle. Prophecy always reminded her of Carl Jung's philosophy regarding nature's affinity: the Hollands satisfied one of the affinities; they lived several doors down from them, both having suburbia French provincials. The family was known to have congenital heart problems with surgeries from babyhood on: now they were dream symbols as was the foreigner left out of the circle crouching in a corner with a fist straddling his privacy: going Dutch? Could a heart problem also be prevalent of a different sort? Could a Frenchman be involved? even Jung might be baffled. And why would I be walking on any stones, much less fieryones? Never would I make a good yogi! What is mother nature signaling to my sub-conscious? Her tension grew as Li opened the toy trunk too adroitly and quickly, hoping to usher them inside the Hotel away from scowling expressions. However, Allie's scrutiny down the side street was too shocking for physical movement, her mouth agape as she stared at a woman hobbling painfully on tiny feet. Lao-po-po (old grandmother,) according to Li. Her heart pounded with sympathy to see this throwback shuffling along the wall for support like a phantom from the Ming Dynasty. Wealthy dowagers expected daughters to be waited on with the ring of a bell or by summoning with the crook of a finger. Even peasants bound their daughter's feet in hopes they would rise to the level of si-mu, (married woman of better class).

This was the very antithesis of Mao's proposal for the working woman: Quotation number thirty-one of the Moa bible was infused in Allie's memory . . . "equality among the sexes, a goal of Communism: multiple burdens which women must shoulder are to be eased." Instead of an embroidered satin shift, this little old dowager wore the same shapeless garment with a mandarin collar that peasants wore, a government issue of drab, dusty blue! Her burden was obviously not being eased, her inheritance dwindled away, or put into a melting pot to share under the leap forward regime.

Allie waved hello to the crowd around them, "Ni hao!" Some waved back reluctantly.

Chapter 2

The hotel room had an inactive steam radiator, causing the Smiths to pull their Angora sweaters more tightly around shivering flesh. At least this shivering was from absence of heat and not from fear of arrest. Barney tramped to warm his big feet, well-clad in Stacy Adams walking shoes. "This bathroom could be labeled oriental with an <u>accidental </u>bath or is it oc`-ci-dental? At least the toilet is western and the tub has big feet." He had vacated the interior, bowing to her, and lisping, "next customer."

They exchanged joke for joke to let off steam. "See the cute pandas chewing up the rush rug; it's a bit thin for such fat creatures!" Allie thought the padded pandas looked too real to be relegated to a flimsy throw rug, unraveling around the edges.

"Come study this propaganda lamp," Barney cried. She paused to scrutinize the black teak-wood lamp-table, trimmed in gold, an orphan or a reproduction from the Ming Dynasty. The sculptured lamp was perched on a crocheted doily. It portrayed a pair of lions facing the electric cord pole. "The base is a cog wheel," commented Barney, "grinding up grain under five stars . . . the lamp-shade doesn't hide the communist stars . . . <u>the regime itself could be</u>

lamp-shady. <u>Hah</u>!" "Oh, we'll help with the grinding once the plant is built or at least eliminate the shoveling of animal and human waste." Barney was too busy studying the thermos to respond. The thermos had white Lotus buds floating on huge green pads. Vertical scrolling was pictographic. "I wonder what the writing says." He growled his own reply in a deep, Bogie voice, "Beware of dysentery!. Boiled. or not, in goes protection." He unscrewed a small vial and plopped a halizone tablet into the questionable thermos. Allie moved to a crucible ink painting of the Great Wall hanging over their boxy Rattan bed. The black gauche was mesmerizing until Barney gently tapped a shoulder and intoned a pleading soprano whine, "Hey, Starlight, let's check out the mess hall; I'm starved!"

"I'll follow you. Bon apatite!"

The only dining room table partially occupied was family size with white linen cloths and napkins. Black porcelain plates and bowls were straddled with chop sticks enameled in black and red on the left and a finger bowl with drying cloth on the right. They chose a setting and pointed to the crystal-colored soda. The white-coat waiter filled their stem ware, then left a menu.

Barney loomed over the airline pilots seated across the table, their caps and uniforms read <u>Japan Air</u>. Barney's ruggedness from earlier days of boxing was softened by dark chestnut eyes. Curious eyes, always questioning. He began slowly. "We're on our way to Tsangchow to build a fertilizer plant." He took a quick sip of the carbonated soda, wondering if he'd said too much, but plowed on anyway . . . "it's in synch with the new reforms: grow your own groceries or join a commune, become a communist. Hah!"

The pilots laughed, rounding and patting their hands, "Fertilizer, eh . . . <u>gou shi</u>, excrement, thought they made their own."

"A big water control project was completed a year ago, so they're more than ready for us to build. We're starting on their anniversary of Communist Founder day, Oct. 1, 1949. We will be launching fireworks! Speaking of '49, that's the same year Chennault wrote his autobiography. Remember the <u>flying tigers?</u>"

"Ah, the Sino-Japanese,'37 to '45. We were born then, but our Dads were American tiger pilots. They taught us to fly." A second look labeled them half-breeds! their Dads were most likely part of the Japanese occupation forces after World War II.

Allie had been humming to herself rubbing her ears, trying to control the ringing . . . we're on our way to San Jose . . . She seized the open pause. "We needed a tiger pilot for a smoother landing. A heavy bump, and swoosh!" She gesticulated with a down sweep of brown, sun-lamp arms. "My first real pain after ear surgery."

"Coming down too fast plays havoc with the inner ear." The second pilot agreed by nodding his head vigorously and shifting in his seat. "They shouldn't have landed like that, even off-schedule with a short runway!" This was the confirmation she needed to plan another route home.

The pilot's main dishes arrived in a flow of steam. They had been toying with their appetizers, finger foods, canapés, chicken broth, drinking Midori liquor. Now they feasted on Japanese tempura and teriyaki, giving their American dining companions ideas for similar orders.

Finally, well-stuffed on Japanese cosine, the grateful pair ambled back to their small hotel room, thankful to sleep away Friday's long jet-lag, knowing they would have a busy Saturday of browsing, shopping, and money changing. Li had arranged for a driver with the Peking Tourist Agency.

Incense was overwhelming, especially sandalwood, even before the driver deposited them at the door of the Friendship Store. He left to locate a safe place for his Toyota.

This was a holiday crowd with greedy, green eyes exchanging moon cakes for the Moon Goddess. "Um ho," the driver muttered, thinking too bad . . . that all days are work days, except for holidays.

A cryptic-labeled door swung open for the pair of breath-holders. A Red Guard used his club to motion them through the bright red portal. They were thankful to be free of the street odor's strange mixture of coal smoke, rotisserie roasting, urine factories, privies. Breathing deeply they drank in the spicy incense odors, Allie with a turned up Nordic nose and Barney with his flat Roman nostrils.

"Our monthly stipend is our spending money; full pay doesn't come until the contract is fulfilled, not until we get home. I suppose a full salary would be too intimidating compared to the low peanuts my fellow coolies earn."

"Wow! what a way to get around the communistic theme of share-and share-alike!"

Barney winked and slapped his change pocket as he motioned to the exchange counter.

Allie nodded, mouthing okay then whisked away, leaving Barney to trade U.S. dollars for Chinese yuan.

She chose hobby essentials: a hog-hair bamboo brush to accompany the sable-hair hake in her luggage for watercolor washes, rice paper and tubes of watercolor paint with a pang of conscience, seeing how much cheaper they were than stateside. Feeling a sense of conspiracy, she thought, "I need to keep as busy as a coolie when not counseling with interpreters." Taking a long look at the small jade tree, the cloisonné` vases, and ginger jars, she mentally book-marked them for a later purchase, if the stipend allowed. The clerk used a framed curiosity, an oblong box of wooden beads strung on wire, to compute an astonishingly low sum of seven Yuan per dollar! Who could argue with that? Her next book-mark for a souvenir was this prehistoric instrument, the abacus! By then, Barney had found her, his pockets bulged with Chinese Yuan as he paid for her purchases.

The day ended still in the throes of jet-lag demanding a long sleep to recuperate. They unpacked their bon voyage gifts, a pair of oriental satin pajamas with French knotted loops and embroidered pockets. Once again, they died to the world.

Chapter 3

The rising sun betrayed its warmth to Ch'in, at least on its capitol city, Peking. It did not deny the Smith's departure date on the wall calendar. Sunbeams dancing on a western calendar with numerical solar months. What a thoughtful gift of the liaison office! No need to struggle over the calligraphy of thirteen lunar months. Nevertheless, the clever propaganda pictures displayed unbounded productivity, season by season, regardless of the revised calendar. Another time keeper, a large clock, displayed the time in calligraphy. "What happened to old fashioned Roman Numerals?" sighed Allie. Barney's "a diller a dollar, a ten o'clock sch . . ." was interrupted by a gentle rap on the door, after which the groggy pair jumped to attention and into traveling clothes. Barney welcomed Li with the Sunday Herald tucked under an arm and travel visas in hand. The Herald, plus their short wave radio, comprised the only connection to the outside world unless something got past their Hong Kong censorship. Special food orders allowed through the company Hong Kong office sometimes contained one or two uncensored magazines.

At the station Barney watched Allie staring down <u>tielu</u>, the iron road. He thought her Einstein eyes must be fascinated to see the tracks come to a single point. Silver tracks, so slick you could use them for a mirror. Her lithe form gave him a deep sense of gratitude making him realize how lonely he would be without her. "Hey, Allie, you look regal in that English suit!" She managed a crooked grin, slumping beneath the shoulder burden of luggage, plus the made-in-Hong Kong reversible coat slung over her left arm.

Barney paced back and forth listening for a whistle from <u>huoche</u>, the fire wagon. He felt both excited. and expectant, thinking of his first train ride on the Sunshine Special across the huge acreage of Texas. El rancho Cima, the Boy Scout retreat, had inaugurated him into the Order of the Arrows. His second train ride he thought would be equally adventurous with better quarters waiting for them than an Indian tepee with a parade ground for a stomping-dance. The new adventure was just miles ahead. He kept tapping his feet, trying to avoid stage fright by humming old jailhouse tunes . . . lean your head *o-ver*, hear the wind blow oh, oh, . . . Did Allie remember to pack her ears with cotton? He switched his tune to . . . O, hand me down my walkin' cane; I'm gonna leave on the midnight train 'cause my sins are take un a-way . . .

He studied their panda-padded torsos, their Mr.& Mrs. sweaters, powder blue cashmeres. Her suit was gabardine, his corduroy. He tucked his thumbs proudly in his home-made belt clinched with a huge turquoise buckle, supporting brown suede trousers. He fingered the lariat tie encircling his collar. Their sweaters were labeled Houston, Texas, as were their passports, stamped and handed over to a Chinese escort. They retained only their green plastic diaries, compliments of the Tourist Agency. Chairman Mao's profile was embedded in a silver emblem surrounded by a red stoplight. The Red Guard station inspectors flipped through the pages, but the Smiths were a step ahead of them keeping the pages blank. They knew that personal comments would arouse suspicion and be confiscated by zealots. Negative opinions branded the author a paper tiger and sentenced him to public service either in the rice paddies or cleaning privies. The over-ambitious, no doubt, recorded the kidnapping of Shang Kai Shek, becoming copiers. So they agreed to use the dairies as address books like graduates leaving school. They'd consider fulfillment of the contract a great graduation gift.

A shrill whistle announced the arrival of <u>huoche</u> with locomotive bell and puffs of steam, loud enough to drown out Allie's "hurrah." Well, it's not an Amtrak or Silver bullet, it's the Indian iron horse." She raised her voice. "I hope it gets us there

23

before sun-down! "Her shouting outlived the steam and caused onlookers to gasp at hearing the strange dialect.

Boosting her up the steps, he sighed. "Yeah, we're off to our brave new jobs. You Pocahontas, me Standish." Barney settled onto a hard coach seat putting an arm around Allie, forgetting one of the pointers in their orientation.(Chinese don't touch in public.*)* She wiggled away, thinking the out-dated custom almost as stupid as pet animals and song birds penned and fattened for food. She wondered if he knew that Pocahontas married John and not Miles as the Chinese would have it—no wedded bliss to control population growth. Soon dozing off by counting the clack, clacks, metal-to-metal noises, Allie reentered the vivid, recurring dream, the neighborly circle with one loner.

She had often dreamed of something about to take place, for example, Pete, her precious parakeet appeared in a vision just as she was dozing off, then fluttered down from his perch. The next morning she found him lifeless, crumpled at the bottom of the cage. Pete's spirit had winged free, letting her know he was leaving, garbed in his same beautiful feathers of Windsor and cerulean blues. Later blues on her palate turned feathers into a "Tribute to Pete," a heart-felt portraiture. This event made the neighborly circle dream less ominous.

As the iron horse raced by making rapid staccato stops, Barney was lost in studying small towns. Even the tiniest villages replicated versions of the Great Wall with peasants living like troglodytes. Each village was closed with a single gate. Plastic sheeting over bamboo frames covered some of the crops. Rice paddies, endless rows of peanuts, apple and pear orchards, pigs in dug-outs, donkeys in harness, slumping with the weight of coal. Even human bearers shouldered heavy pots on bamboo poles. "Is that a compressor or a water pump?" Allie had aroused from dreamland.

"Either one could go with our Urea plant, whatever contraption it is!" he muttered to the sleepy head.

Streaming sights of shot-gun houses connected with Allie's drowsy vision as the train braved a steep hill overlooking the village. Like Peking flats, some had bamboo roofing with a second family living upstairs and climbing an outside ladder. Comparing to Japan, Allie had eye-sketched tile roofing and pagoda-shaped homes. She wondered if the Chinese sat on the floor also; she hoped not.

Passing vistas and recent memoirs ground to a halt as the conductor's booming voice announced their new home town, "Tsangchow!"

With a long step down they exited their version of the Orient Express, having finally agreed on a name, even though it mimicked an old movie. They displayed their most exuberant smiles for the welcome mat of quick shadowy smiles and bowed heads. Taken together, they formed a template with cut-outs of red-star caps and decorated chests. These escort-identical ushered the Smiths into an official van with its giant star on the side door. A crescent and star flag waved from the hood. She took comfort in knowing that their coffin box was stored in the rear. Barney's wooden trunk that touting friends thought resembled a coffin had safely landed on foreign soil.

Despite a misty chill in the air, the sun looked twice as high on this opposite side of the earth. The driver parked in a circular drive in front of a flat-roofed three-story guest house. It dawned on the astonished pair that this house was a replica of Mao Zedong's compound, as pictured midway in the seam of their dairies. His portrait adorned the apex of the compound as well as a kite displaying calligraphy. When would it be allowed to fly? Allie pondered. What propaganda was this? But it was the smell of roses and the wide range of colors that brought a smile to Allie's face and caused her eyes to twinkle. Roses were the centerpiece of the circular drive, her favorite subject for a watercolor floral. She would washed in every color, from ecru to vermillion, talisman to pink, scarlet to darkest red. Exotic iris, chrysanthemums, peonies, and carnations smiled in greeting from their huge clay pots and flower beds surrounding the perimeter of the Friendship House. Her right hand itched to feel the soft-bristle hake stroking washes, the bamboo hog-bristle overlaying petals and leaves. She thought of the football mums her senior home room gave her to wear to the Friday night game. Though it seemed like years ago, she recreated the ease of blocking it off in oils. Not an art teacher; nevertheless, art was her passion, her center of expression for lonely evenings when Barney would be doing field work. So now, another life had begun as Barney nudged her toward the entry of their new field of work.

A Red Guard rushed ahead to open the heavy red door, then a houseboy grabbed their luggage and dashed for the stairs. "Oh no!" cried the gwai-lo. She was western and soft-featured but looked like the foreign devil of Pearl Buck and Elizabeth Lewis, appearing as fast as a phantom in a pink satin dressing gown, hair curlers dangling, "they will stay next door to us." She pointed a pink manicured forefinger to the door beside her. The white-coated houseboy looked wide-eyed with mouth open, but did as she commanded. With no other suite available on the first floor, the boy outfitted two rooms some distance apart, both with an old fashioned massive tub, and thankfully, a western toilet. The double windows with bars, opened onto a midget balcony. She could use one bedroom for painting or meeting guests.

So orders come before introductions! What goes on here? Both Allie and Barney had the same thought, staring inquiringly at the late-sleeper, the all-of-a-sudden apparition.

The pink curlers introduced herself only after her subterfuge was carried out. "I'm the site rep's wife." She extended her hand to Barney who noticed the manicured nails, long enough for a Chinese scholar if any remained. "Leora Mueller . . . Luke and I have been expecting you; do you play Mahjong or Cribbage?"

"No, but we could learn," Barney spoke, and Allie nodded affirmatively. It was a week later that Leora's trickery came to light. An Amsterdam pair arrived and took the Smith's sumptuous second-floor suite, at least sumptuous according to the available resources. A tall gaunt elderly and a younger genteel settled in and opened their windows no matter how cold, explaining their need for fresh air, and no wonder, considering how often they lit up their fags.

Allie was as mad as a hornet's nest. Stomping her Hush Puppy loafers didn't release the pent-up anger so she did a dozen jumping jacks. There was nothing to throw but a hand mirror, but holding it high she caught sight of the painting on the backside. She cried, "Vanity, vanity, all is vanity! Oh Azna, where is my poise? "It had been a week of hugging the big bulb over the Mahjong table sneaked in from bribing the houseboy. An outright defiance of the mid-October date for starting electricity. Allie found it hard to forgive Leora. She tried to imagine Leora's month of loneliness, then the joy of having a pair of fellow Americans for company. She knew how to manipulate! The lost suite was a spacious rotunda with a fireplace. How comfortable they would have been in one unit instead of two separated rooms, forming an improvised suite. She felt sheepish noticing the backside of the hand mirror. A painting of the barefoot doctor dismounting her bicycle to administer to a line of children. Analyzing the painting subdued her temper. A farmer with a rake over his shoulder was looking on, smiling. Another smiling figure on the sideline resembled Chairman Mao, the champion of peasantry! The small, but well-silvered mirror was outlined with willow trees and herbs, symbolic of healing. This hand mirror folded and locked to support shaving. It was Barney's only looking glass, their first purchase at a local store. Guest house officials had to close the store to the public's curious eyes peering in through available cracks and windows. Westerners were strange looking, maybe gwai-lo, foreign devils. The toy section drew her like a magnet, like the rebounding yo-yo always a part of acrobatic acts. The pair of sticks joined by twine would demand speedy twirling for a rebound. She would give it a try. Harmonicas would not be attempted, but would make exciting gifts for itinerant farm children she had tutored. Not too different from the peasants on the back of the mirror! Plastic animal shapes, zebra, lion, dragon, bear, turned into mouth organs. Small chalk boards caught her eye; they were made of real slate, though only carpenter markers were available, not stateside chalk. What a great item for her toll painting class for rural landscapes, especially a snow scene, then looking out a dark window . . . as Jung's affinity of all things would have it, the sky had turned bleak enough for a Chinese snow. She doubted that any winter sports would be allowed, even with a slowing down of the work schedule.

A yellow cotton dress stretched out and pinned to the wall was a must; as no other clothing was available. Since only children wore dresses, this dress had to be made for an older child, perhaps a teenager, but it fit Allie's size 10-12 figure according to the estimate when held up in front.

Thinking of the dress reminded her to choose something for tonight's banquet. Anger aside, she felt completely subdued as she chose a form-fitting navy blue pant suit with a hip length tunic sporting white cuffs and collar. She knotted the cloth belt to hang saucily on the left side.

Demurely following behind Barney, they were motioned to their seats in a massive dining hall that would be completely bare except for the flag stand and a mural of the Great Wall, hand painted in black ink exactly like the one in the Peking Hotel, they'd admired one month ago. The long table was replete with fresh vegetable casseroles, a goose turned upside down like the earth itself, she thought, envisioning her family living on the earth's opposite parallel getting up for breakfast or going to work. Dessert here came first instead of last then a strong Molokai toast for friendship and job success. All cried <u>gan bey</u>! or bottoms up in Mandarin Chinese. Barney and Allie had been eyeing bottles of the crystal colored soda and quickly dashed an already opened one into their stem ware. They beamed their widest oriental smiles meaning, we're not being inhospitable. But up jumped the dragon a guest house counselor walking behind them with toast in hand, "Why you not drink good Molokai?"

The school mum in Allie was quick to reply, "We Americans are inclined to take after Edgar Allen Poe . . . . alcoholic poet?" Adroitly changing the subject, she pointed to the fancy carving, a centerpiece of fresh vegetables honed into flowers. "How lovely! soo Poe-etic." She swallowed, then ducked her head, remembering that book burning here had probably included Poe's poetry. Barney's face relaxed as they sipped their sweet lime-flavored soda, relieved to see the official saunter down the long diplomatic table. He had ignored the Amsterdam engineers to wind up behind Luke and Leora, a pair of opposites: feminine plumpness with a freckled face already flushed and red under dyed dish water tresses. Luke was

31

tall and limber, looking of his sixty years trying to hold his share of Poe but lisping and leaning on his interpreter. Allie pondered the outcome of banqueting over a long period of time, only to turn into an alcoholic and stagger through a terminal job. Poor Luke! The same fate as Mee-ster Jordan of Li's description.

The final toast of the evening was to Chairman Moa Zedong's health, his long illness, as described, seemed related to the American version of Lou Garrick Disease. A terminal illness.

Following the last toast, the intemperate pair made their way down the dark hall to the sanctity of their room for a restless night. There was much to ponder.

Chapter 4

Allie awoke clapping hands over ringing ears. The loud speaker made her wonder how many Chinese would be sharing her intensity deafness. It wasn't the piped in sound system of a public school, pledging allegiance to the flag or saying a morning prayer. The sound system came from outside, permeating thin walls with blaring martial drums and bamboo flutes reminding Americana of Arkansas folk music. The added pipe with only four strings made it distinctively Chinese. How she loved this sound, though it was a rude reminder of still being in the People's Republic. The high-twang instructions of the announcer relaying what to do, where to go, then the propaganda news, mostly incomprehensible to her limited Sino-vocabulary; but the only other choice was to read the large public scrolls in calligraphy. There were small billboards under glass stationed along thoroughfares. What a far cry from earlier days, when Huang Di taught Taoism's simple philosophy of wholesome living . . . one-hundred years for him, preceding his turning into a dragon and flying away to Heaven. "Go with the flow," preached this first Emperor.

Despite the ear ringing, Allie could figured out some of the Mandarin dialect's rousting demands for tai chi, already in progress, ci ke, The forest clearing, Zhao ze, meant the glen. Wasn't this by the deserted homestead? From the window it looked to be flanked by endless rows of cabbage, bot soy, and wheat fields. A clearing was deliberately left, or a glen where nothing grew except the soft foot prints over a period of time with the slow pounding of tai chi.

She yawned thinking another snooze would be restful, denying a "go with the flow." Barney was already in the shower and his interpreter at the door was calling their names, "Al-ee, Barn-ee." Her dainty stature was not unlike the smooth butter-skin electricians climbing poles, and with no one's permission, turning into photons in Allie's camera. (She did a lot of secret photography, tou pai, from the one window that folded out its bars to frame the midget balcony, so uniquely Chinese. Who said these inventors had stopped inventing?) In reality, the amateur electricians were educators serving their two outdoor-years as outlined by Mao's alternating white-shirt, blue-shirt policy. Was this his attempt to round-out society, making his store-front manikins into cliff-hanging dummies or sand-paper lumber-jacks?

Ma Le stood nakedly exposed to Allie's internal scrutiny as she entered and went directly to the book shelf. Having been educated in England, her language was crisp and well-articulated . . . She was married, and had one child. Only <u>YUT</u>, was allowed, unless female. Since Ma Le's one child was female, she was allowed to try again for a son, that is, if she were able to sleep with her handsome Tyan. They were not even permitted to travel on the same tour, despite numerous <u>gwai-lo</u>, requests. In other words, expatriates were campaigning for this popular couple. She had proudly brandished a picture of Tyan in a Shanghai school group, with a whispered explanation, "Education has to take a back seat because of food shortage." Shrugging her shoulders nonchalantly, she added, "The peasant farmer is lord and master, for now."

"Is that what they mean by the cultural revolution? Children working in fields or else becoming Red Guards?" Allie's tone was sincere as she probed, with one-eye cocked.

"They can earn a scholarship to college by working in the fields and diligently growing good crops, <u>chiao-liu ching-yen</u>, observing advanced production brigades. Poverty is the dragon we have to slay."

Methodology appeared cruel, harshly denying private ownership. Allie thought the communists needed to take a step backward to reset or shift gears to forward, allowing some private ownership, some persona, like the barefoot doctor's personal attention. Quite the opposite of the feeling all must have of being a can in a can factory.

The water boy slipped in the usual giant thermos and quickly retreated, ignoring Ma Le's thumbing through a western magazine. A furtive glance would have exposed Hong Kong's heavily deleted advertising, thrust away by black markers, not to preclude any other exposure censors thought under-minded the present regime. With small soft hands and soulful oohs and ahs, she flipped pages while waiting for Barney. When Barney arrived, Ma Le walked the Smiths to the dining room, then took her leave waving good-by to Barney, "See you at the job site. Joy geen,"

With chopsticks clicking they tackled scrambled eggs, egg rolls, and a soy bean-chick pea-peanut concoction. "Egg rolls have to be stuffed with pork," Allie commented, "considering the back-yard pig-sty dugouts."

"And don't forget the oink-oinks that keep us awake on moony nights." He ended his sentence with a groan at the pungent smell of fresh bread coming from one of the huge iron ovens in the kitchen. The group as a whole had basked in the dark warmth as they were led through the kitchen for a one-time look at the massive iron stoves heated with coal. While the savory smell of bread whetted his appetite, like a good boy, he would have to eat his rice cakes.

Each diner ordered his own choices if he could make out the pinyin phonetics, far easier to decipher than the traditional calligraphy that harbored no phonetics. Each unit of strokes, supposed to represent a place or an event, looked as indefinite as a scrambled egg. Allie thought of the first day of Elementary Ed when a picture was shown the class accompanied by familiar symbols such as triangles, squares, and hearts. The future teachers were expected to encode the symbols. "This is how a child learns to read," explained their professor. "You are luckier to have an illustration to go by, plus adult insight." Menu-reading seemed destined to become a similar procedure, a continuous education.

The waiter appeared with a ewer of green tea, pouring and replacing the padded cover. They would have to put to rest thoughts of espresso, milk or any milk product. Shaking his head to Barney's request, <u>mian bao</u>? fresh bread, alas, was being baked for dinner.

Name-plates had been prepared for each couple in English, though small calligraphy was beneath each name. A long banquet table was set up for single short-term operators. The kitchen staff was easily recognizable by their stiff white Mandarin-collared tunics. Visiting workers wore khakis and jeans; the ladies western-style pant-suits gave the dining room its lay-out of the work-a-day world. She grinned to remember a finger pointing at Barney on the train accompanied one slurring word, "cow-y-boy!" She had answered back, "<u>Ma shang</u>," get on your horse.

While studying the diners, she nonchalantly grabbed at peanuts with chopsticks, lazily noticing a door swing open for a uniformed house boy. He was waving a neatly folded yellow trench coat like a May Day kite. She chocked on a peanut and groaned, "<u>Aw geh</u> . . . <u>um goy</u>," mine . . . please. She hadn't even missed the coat, "<u>Duo xie` ni,!</u>" thank you very much to which the attendant nodded in reply handing her the coat, "<u>bu yong xie`</u>," you're welcome. She blamed her over-stuffing in the English wool suit, too warm to miss another garment. No wonder she left it on the train, but only in present day China would it be dutifully returned. Ah, the rigid discipline! Packing a year's supply of personal belongings made a lot to tote about, having been informed of "being your own bellhop; to each his own" was preached by Mao as he parted people and jobs, sending scholars into fields for peasant labor. Tote your own belongings; be a responsible citizen. Communism was a strange kind of equality, an enforced brotherhood. But Allie's spiritual belief was more like rotating lifetimes, the wheel of rebirth, balancing out the personality. She believed she had already spent a Chinese advent. Deja vou, included affinity with the over-sized bathtub. Whom could she reward? "Neither a lender nor a borrower be . . . not even a needle and thread" according to Mao. What about gift-giving? she would plan to leave something behind, perhaps paintings. For now, her big smile and nod she hoped was appropriate. She couldn't help but wonder if the label, "made in Hong Kong," influenced its return. One had to go back several dynasties to come up with Confucius saying that men are brothers in the four seas. She had only to return to last Saturday to understand the on-going result of this saying. The dark room for movie-viewing depicted the Long March of 1949 after losing Taiwan. This was not an Oklahoma trail of tears but a laughing troop of Mao Zedong's young Red Guards.

Entreprenuers, as well as guest house staffers, were shifting uncomfortably on metal folding chairs. Old mores of dynastic days seemed drastically revised. Marching along singing propaganda lyrics, the esprit de corps for the new young China brought a barely perceptible groan from the subdued audience. Chiang Kai-shek had been chased to Taiwan. Political songs were sonorous longings for lost brothers which included the territories bordering China. The iron fists of the Chinese were wearing silk gloves, for now.

After the movie a trailer glorified the peasant for his education in agriculture, promising a college scholarship, as Ma Le had explained, to anyone who excelled or made a contribution to growing and marketing, a so-called basic militia unit, chi-kan, min-ping Teachers who taught the classics were punished in various shameful ways. It was hard to imagine a student punishing a teacher! It seemed that Red Guard pupils misused their ping-pong paddles. What skillful manipulators! thought Allie, misleading simple-minded villagers, using land reform to persuade support for collectivization, eventually organizing into communes with the Government confiscating the land. Sharing the wealth, however, proved more profitable than managing a small plot subject to natural disaster, a flood or even an earthquake. Poor villagers under Japanese rule prior to the communist take-over were lucky if they had kaoliang <u>ping-tzu</u> every day, millet flour mixed with chaff. Droughts, famines, or locusts could reduce the diet to elm-bark powder, seed, and leaf, or a gruel of millet with beans and vegetables called <u>tou-tsai-fan</u>. Salty white turnips or carrots, not meat, served as main dishes.

Grateful for a decent breakfast, Allie folded the yellow trench over her arm and accompanied Barney to the door and to the company bus, waving good by. It was Monday, the first day of a six-day work week. Ma Le simultaneously waved to Allie from the official Tsangchow limousine. Vehicles switching gears seem to sing, men are brothers in the four seas.

Chapter 5

Popping up behind her, Leora suggested a morning excursion. A small grove of Eucalyptus trees confirmed her vision of tai chi arms and legs suspended in air, pausing, listening to the sounds of nature. Only silence prevailed, as pets and birds had already become food items. The voiceless bunny would meet the profound silence of nature if he were still around. A sort of parallel was entering her conscience We are not too different, she thought, feeling a strong kinship with the balancing exercise, as it related to recent inner ear surgery.

Nodding toward the forlorn mansion, Leora studied the French provincial decor then voiced a conclusion. "I'll bet this abandoned estate was a thriving cotton plantation . . . but along came the Boxer Revolt . . . remember your world history text . . ."

"Oh yes!" interrupted Allie, "I do remember. The French retreating from Tientsin. Some probably came to about where we are now. I noticed cotton on the forbidden items list; it now comes here from the U.S. We have to get permission to buy back our cotton. Dan wei means give permission." Allie recalled the massive sell-out of American dry goods stores. She'd love to purchase more yardage

41

to add to her already bulging cedar chest. A new electric Singer was ready and waiting.

"The only French I've seen in China work in the hair saloon in Peking. If you can stand cold water, they do a fabulous job which reminds me I have asked for a cold wave kit; I'll holler when it arrives. Oh, and by-the-way, "she whirled around mysteriously, putting a pink finger of silence to her matching pink mouth, "I've been tipped off about our next unscheduled business tour It's where our supply ship docks, the Port of Tientsin! Commies have to pave the way the same as they do when we shop local; you know the great job they do emptying the store of prying eyes." Leona raised her mascara brows in a mocking gesture.

"Maybe more dangerous eyes stalk our tour bus." Allie wide-eyed back.

Their walking tour ended at the rear door of the guest house. Both nodded to the Guard. Then Leora motioned to the last room. "They call this our <u>chu</u>, a sort of kitchen where supplies are brought from Hong Kong. Our company purchases a few choices, mainly Tang, cheese, canned ham, peanut butter, sardines, and crackers, even coffee! We pass them around . . . " Once more she turned to Allie, trailing close behind, to make a point of her second conclusion, "If we admire some dish at a banquet, they will add it to our menu."

The next Hong Kong arrival wasn't food but a vintage contraption, resembling the first ever of permanent waving machines. Leora backed off with a look of frustration. Allie came to her rescue offering to be the first guinea pig. She glanced at a shipping label. Ah ha, the Ambassador Hotel Beauty Saloon has gotten rid of a relic. The solution was applied by a serious looking madam with black hair, as straight as broom straws made of black-bristle hog hair. The timer was set for 40 minutes, a slow bake and voila, Allie was released with Mae Murray curls. She felt like a refugee from silent movies, smelling like ammonia, but happy to be as kinky as her Mother and sister, Sandy, both born as curly as black pica-ninnies.

Holland looked askance and muttered that her hair looked burnt. He was entering a Toyota and offering her a ride to town.

"Maybe next time," she waved him on, thinking what a treat it would be to go on a shopping spree with the handsome Grecian featured, slightly freckled, Hans. Could he be the guy crouching in the corner of her dream? . . . the international circle's Holland symbol, all linking hands except his. She still wondered why.

After a week, Allie washed the smelly ammonia out of her hair, admiring the golden curls in the plastic hand mirror Barney had left folded from his morning shave. The word permanent to her thinking

43

became simultaneous with Chinese inventiveness and the "made in China" labels.

The hair played a leading role in a camera flick. Not only the hair, but she, herself, vanishing into thin air between two dark haired lady-welders. These ladies resembled the porcelain faces, the orange-skin dolls, climbing poles and manning tools on the job site, fulfilling the job-switching indoor-to-outdoor. The resemblance ended there, as these clear-cut ladies had redder faces from manning a welding rod, in fact, they were Barney's pupils who requested a picture taken with her. Allie's yellow dress and platinum gold hair contending with yellow walls . . . and camera light, denied any trace of her body form. She was a blank between two burly welders on the processed celluloid of her Polaroid camera, now leaving open-mouthed viewers to ponder over the magic photons of light banishing her into thin air.

The garment, purchased in town, may have been meant for a teenager daring to escape the new leap-forward dress code; however, it was a perfect fit for Allie, as well as an unintended camouflage. Pearl buttons to waist, a belt that buttoned in back, a peter pan collar, and pleated skirt, a simple, everyday wear. Not even a pearl button could be seen in the Polaroid snapshot. She would save the dress for oncoming holiday celebrations and save the picture to show the hecklers at home who teased Barney about his coffin box.

The green corduroy jumpsuit would do fine to show off her new curls, but she wondered how appropriate it would be for today's unknown destination. Her navy pant suit was usually chosen for touring, but was now in a laundry cart. Only after boarding the bus was the group informed that they were headed: for the People's Republic Art Institute The guides noticed her beaming with excitement, and upon arrival, introduced her as a famous American artist . . . ah, the protocol at work!

Cloisonné demonstration was a lesson in patience. Allie tip-toed as if walking on eggs, awe-stricken over the process. An ancient design was poured into moldings, pigment, after pigment, layer upon layer, each a separate firing. Time did not matter, just the finished product. Now she understood what made cloisonné` so special. Both Allie and Barney had purchased small cloisonné vases for seventy Yuan or $10; they would cost at least $100 in Houston, larger ones going into thousands . . . They had priced these treasures in the new Memorial Maul while shopping for personal items to pack, opting to leave room for artifacts.

Allie moved on to a more remote booth for another lesson in patience. A young girl wearing a ponytail half-stood poring over a glass snuff bottle. There was no room for error. The challenge was stroking inside the glass bottle, painting the scene up-side-down. Allie stood motionless, staring at the artist's slender hands doing a single, steady stroke; her face taut in deep concentration. Time fading into eternity, the art form going back to the 17th century, to Marco Polo's presentation to the Emperor. Since then Chinese imitators included jade, brass, ivory, wood and porcelain. The memorized pattern required steady skill, no originality allowed. Just like the dress code adorning the artists. Loose fitting government pants and tunics left no room for individuality, unless a scarf or headband served to identify each clone. Allie wondered if her green jumpsuit was noticed?

Moving on from snuff bottle tension, several students were laughing and hollering bu hao, (ouch!) as they applied straight pins to secure a square of silk. How they would love map pins! Could map pins be something they failed to invent? Their stiff white silk formed a background for the fritters in an Iris garden; another square of silk accommodated a pair of mating finch encircling plum blossoms. "Oh, what a dilly!" exclaimed Allie, remembering a worn-out cliché. The girls looked startled but went on grinding crucible ink, egg yolk, and powdered pigments, a water mix, similar to fast-drying acrylic. This would mesmerize any amateur. Their silk could be purchased in the Friendship Store. She added this to her mental lisr of gift items along with rolled-up tapestries and embroidered pillow tops. Let Mom and Sandy mull over the standard calligraphy: a message always accompanied the signature. Authentic snuff bottles were understandably high-priced, beyond the stipend budget. Limited pay still hung over their heads, like the Sword of Damocles; however, the twenty dollar sale flashed in her mind. A pair of fast-moving specialist, having no time for shopping finagled their two cloisonné vases. After many ohs and ahs and downright begging, the Smiths gave in and said good by to the two vases, intended for gifts. They would bide their time for another monthly stipend and another secret tour. One had to be naively trusting like rolling the drums slowly on the narrow streets of Laredo. Allie had never been happy with surprises, but their hosts were bending her mind by wearing their worm-silk gloves.

Chapter 6

Since camera owners were rare, the <u>gwai-lo</u> guests were incessantly snapping Polaroid's and giving the excited posers a snapshot of themselves. Then Allie was faced with a whole class of interpreters from the Peking University. Ma Le said they would be happy to pose for a group picture. A passer-by was drafted so Allie could be included in the snapshot.

"My pupils only want to study your voice."

Ad lib speeches went well until Allie was handed a list of collected expressions heard on the job site. With her mouth wide open, she turned fiery red with embarrassment. How could she ad lib . . . indecent language? No, they had to let off steam with the worst expletives they could conjure. Hell and damnation, <u>gai si</u> and <u>ma da</u> didn't sound too bad, but bathroom slang had to go! According to Ma Le, bullshit is <u>Hu shuo bu dab</u>, and fuck is <u>Kao</u>! Measuring their sex organ in the company latrine was ridiculous, she thought, turning more red-faced. The black book of Shanghai and Hong Kong names belonged to Hans. She recalled his offering the tiny tattered keepsake to single guys if they chose Hong Kong's wonk, or Susie Wong's girlie bars during their R &R's. He had to be the corner-crouch in her vivid dream. Stamping her feet, she vowed to make a dunce cap and smash it on his head. On second thought, being an incessant traveler and offering his girlie dossier, he knew the girls were probably smaller than their foreign baits and felt free to charge more. What a dilemma! She felt like one of the phrases, pissed off! <u>Xiao bia.</u>

Mind-bending comes from many directions. No wonder, she thought, the Ugly American isn't allowed inside the University of Peking, even for a visit.

Waving <u>zu jian,</u> good bye, to the students she promised <u>ming tian,</u> tomorrow, we will discuss better English. After all, they only wanted to hear her voice, but her voice didn't seem like her own.

The chance to confront Hans came and went unexpectedly. The Brussels aspect had requested a Thanksgiving dinner to be observed in their tradition with Gouda cheese and grape wine from the Netherlands. The cake was an artistic crown with candles honoring Queen Juliana. Questions fired at the Dutch included, "Why are you working in China?"

"Our itch to travel is more important now than ever. Our country is flooded with immigrants from Surinam; inflation is rampant." Hans did well as a speaker while Barney held up a middle finger, "One apple costs one American dollar. "We had walked around the square on our stopover in Amsterdam. A boat ride on the canal was beyond reach, but Allie walked through art museums and toured a dairy farm to sketch a windmill."

She recalled one of her father's stories about the second world war. The neutral Netherlands saved many downed pilots hiding them and offering their meager fare. The country became a charter member of the United Nations . . . . and, oh yes, boy friends were allowed to sleep on the sofa until a permanent relationship emerged . . . this last she was sure she had read in a ladies magazine.

She softened toward blue-eyed Hans with a twinkle in his eyes as he offered friendship, chess games, and recorded music to who came to his room on non-working days. She asked if he had a picture of a windmill for her to paint. He pondered a moment then nodded yes.

Following Thanksgiving, the next celebration was a job site occasion called the Raising of the Winch. A steel cylinder was mechanically hoisted to stabilize the construction tower. Many tall slender derricks were attached to electric poles. It was as if suddenly the fields of non-fertile soil had turned into a world of metal scaffolding soon to supply jump-start chemistry to speed the growth of wheat and edible vegetables.

A long table was set up for viewers, mindless of the chill. Dignitaries and expatriates shivered under layers of clothing sipping the traditional green tea. Standing behind was an endless sea of faces lined against the high wall. Enormous newly scrolled pictographs decorated the brick building. With every sip the white coats added more tea. Picture taking was allowed, in fact, welcomed in a job setting, out to wield a place in the world's economy. Mao had written, "not all foreigners are bad; some are good, some are bad." Failure of his leap forward could be blamed on a denial of trained engineers. President Nixon's visit in 1972 upgraded their step forward.

The successful winch-raising was met with cheers and toasting. Allie shivered under her layers of double-knit long johns, dark blue wool pants and a white fleece-lined turtle neck t-shirt. A camel's hair sweater was topped with her reversible trench. She also wore a hand-knit ear muff skull cap from Aunt Nell's gift shop and worsted gloves from Levy's, her two favorite hometown stores. She still felt numb as she stiffly walked to the bus and back to her room in the Guest House. She grimaced to recall the houseboy wearing only a starched, white coat adding more tea after every sip. She had grown to like the strange unique taste, though a pair of limeys had offered her black English tea, with a game of chess. She soon found that they were experts, way beyond her ability to concentrate. The outdoor ring toss with houseboys was more her level.

Table tennis was always available if up to matching with nimble fingered Chinese whose nails were now well-trimmed, no longer allowed to grow inches long. Even basketball was on-going if only they wouldn't insist that guests only should be allowed to win. Were they trying to show us that face-saving no longer meant winning.

Intrigued by one player, she recalled asking the interpreter on duty about his strange black eyes that turned up at the corners and were much larger than other oriental's. Indeed, he seemed from outer space. But no, he was dubbed Mongolian, from Outer Mongolia, not lately from Mars.

Thinking of exercise made her long to chase a ball or swing a paddle to limber up her stiff limbs, but another human enigma had been escorted to her quarters. A pair of blue-gray occidental eyes, a small heavy-set traveler had successfully crossed the Mongolian dessert and was introduced to Allie as Morris Turner.

Western-dressed in a black-worsted suit, he seemed out of context as he sobbed out his stressful story. "I-I've been threatened and scorned . . . is it my suit? My eyes? Why do they hate me so?" He retrieved a white linen handkerchief from a vest pocket and slunk down in one of the two cushioned cane backs that Allie motioned to.

"I think it's where you have been. You could be considered a spy of the tribal Qui, since you're not wearing the typical gray or navy drabs. Stay between our men on your way to Peking. They are prizes, well guarded for their engineering skill. Some peasants have been reared to mistrust foreigners ever since the 1900 Boxer Revolt. However, wives are no longer beaten nor concubines allowed. Children are no longer taught to steal from the rich. Before Mao's regime, unpaid soldiers had a choice between theft and starvation. Moa has elevated the peasant to Khubla Khan's pedestal, though still branding his charges 'ignorant-defensive.' A negative dichotomy to say the least!"

Allie wondered if Morris had obtained permission from the home office in Houston to take this route. His home, Sparta, Texas, lies only a few miles south of the Houston office; he could have been a former employee. She hesitated to probe, preferring to think of him as a nice guy desperate to get home; she would file this enigma away with the daily routine.

Following the winch-raising ceremony Ma Le stopped by to say <u>Joy geen</u>, good by. She was headed for the Shanghai Express, pregnant with her second child. Since the first was female, she is allowed another child. Medics expected complications if the fetus did not turn head downward, there could be a breach-positioned birth. Besides, Shanghai was her own birth home.

She batted back the tears and seated her enlarged form in the desk chair that Barney vacated for her. She scanned through a few pages of the new text Bible on the desk before replying in a whisper, "I believe in life after death . . . a few Christians and Buddhists may still be hiding in the old caves near Liaoyang. I think some have escaped the labor enforcement."

Barney straddled a folding side chair, putting on his eye-piercing curiosity. "What transpires after Mao's terminal illness? Is anyone waiting in the shadows?"

She wriggled her hands, suggesting an undercurrent: It will be moderate versus radical, dangerous to Mao's second wife, Jiang Qing, with the gang of four. A military successor is waiting to step in. Hua is moderate, but can he stabilize politics?" She turned to the biblical sermon on the mount and answered her own question, "Yes, I trust that Hua is the answer to prayer."

Chapter 7

The minibus heading for Peking's elementary demonstration school resembled the Americana that plowed into a clothes line pole at Allie's Head Start Center. The head teacher had missed the low curb and whirled into a back yard; the pole was a rude stop sign and the jerk caused Allie to suffer a painful whip-lashed neck. Was the head teacher frustrated because she had replaced Allie from the driver's seat. The switching was an order from the central director who just happened to be present? Allie was used to picking up and tutoring difficult children, but that day's protocol went awry by ego's goo-goo eyes for a pretty Latin face. Today, on this Tsangchow minibus she could relax with a tour driver, sit back without a neck brace, and view the sights of Peking's inner city with several other newcomers and of course, Leora and Luke. Barney was propped up in bed with a swollen leg, mysteriously injured on the job site, at least that is where the swelling began.

The elementary school was expecting visitors and put on their best showmanship. Though not a typical desk-per-pupil routine, each child loved showing off his slate of calligraphy. What would be missing from the home front . . . a refrigerator with the Chinese invented magnet to hold down his art for display. Such magnets are now on U.S. soil, as well as scarce refrigerators. The children's written characters in calligraphy was a common bond with no dialect problem, thanks to the last take-over, the Hans . . . and Confucius who said, "One picture is worth a thousand words." Mandarin or Putonghua was now standard. The spoken word was a different story.

Allie counted at least six dialects of their many ethnic groups, their babbling could have amounted to forty-one minority languages. When a whistle blew, the children lined up for the dragon performance and the political sing-song: "O, long lost brothers of Taiwan or the red rose is Mao . . ." At last, a synthesis, thanks to poetic Mao's music. Allie counted the anomalies: first, the carpenter markers the children were using with no white chalk available, reminding her of the real chalk at home for the leave-a-note plaques she would be making from the slates she'd purchased. Second, The Little Red Book, beyond childhood comprehension, yet carried around by everyone, including herself: their Communist Bible, The Sayings of Mao, patterned after The Communist Manifesto with some essence of Confucius or Lao-tzu, despite the inflamed hatred of classics, to wit, the book burnings.

A third anomaly, the pandering of Red Guards being sworn in at a very early age. Some didn't appear to be over twelve years, shouldering spears, garbed in gray uniforms, and duck-billed caps centered by a red star. Their arm bands displayed another red star, rhythmically swinging left and right alongside knickerbockers trousers, leggings over sandals. The seeds of propaganda were still sown, though Moa was in danger of being relegated to billboards with his portrait floating in clouds instead of hanging in every town hall throughout China. His terminal illness could reverse these impractical anomalies.

Allie prayed that their small group of foreign observers would become an overture, reaching out to rescue these vulnerable children from mediocrity. Their ancestral talent for invention needed to catch up with modern technology. Droopy eyes with dark round pupils and pink-fleshed faces looked apathetic. She longed to coddle the infants and give them a new outlook. Don't touch! guardian hands waved her away, glinting their widened eyes.

Upon glancing around at the international faces, one young man looked familiar. She was sure to have seen this round, feminine-soft face in a company newspaper, though his bright blue eyes were not evident in newsprint. His pregnant wife had been hit by glass from a tornado; he, no doubt, was here earning money for medical treatment as well as home repairs. Racking her brain for his name, she finally ventured, "Michael? Aren't you the expectant father?"

"I sure hope so, did you see the write-up? My wife's in a wheel chair, but doing okay with one month to go." Nodding toward the children, he leaned toward her and whispered before passing by, "We're better off than these rascals. Eh?" She nodded back, wishing Barney had taken the tour instead of being propped up in bed with a swollen leg or even worse, soaking in a tub of ill-smelling herbs. He didn't think he was hurt on the job site as the Chinese claimed. She made a mental note of looking around the bedroom for some insect. Ma Le had whispered, "Look out for the fiddler spider," gesturing for silence after painting a fiddle in the air, knowing her people were super-sensitive about saving face.

Allie knew Ma Le would not be missed on this tour due to the banning of a visit to her university, even though her daughter could be ensconced in the crowd of elementary school performers. Her departure to Shanghai had been met with nay-sayers who thought Tyan should accompany her. Finally after much debate, he was allowed to go. Foreign interference was already beginning to foment. Would there be a revival of the Boxer Secret Society to expunge foreign influence? She looked over her shoulder wondering if the small daughter really was in the crowd. Not only was the Peking University off-limit, but also the Temple of Heaven. From a distance Allie noticed a repair unit at work. Turning to Leora, she remarked, "I hope that lathe is turning over a new leaf . . . more power to old times! <u>Ganbei</u> to the lunar New Year!" She did a mock toast, pretending to gulp down the fiery Molokai, knowing in reality, she could never do so.

The domed-shaped pagoda with ornate panels made a perfect circle with a blue triple roof that resembled a wedding cake. Since weddings weren't encouraged just now, tradition would opt for the resemblance of three overlaid fans ending with a glistening ornamental b-shaped top

White steps leading up to the entrance meant closed doors, <u>guan men </u>(construction site) <u>gong di</u> (repairing): another form of face-saving was to lavish perfection. She dared a Polaroid shot to file away in her art-scrap file next to the mysterious iron lion she had snapped near Tsangchow. This was a strange, mythical creature, probably Jurassic, the size of a dinosaur with a large round vat on its back. Several dug-out steps defined it as ceremonial. What sacrifices were performed? She shuttered to think of herself with her head touching the animal belly instead of sitting on a ledge in Barney's snapshot. Iron Lion, indeed! How did it escape the melt-down of iron for weapons? With a semblance of wings and a curved beak, perhaps it could be a Griffin, but the thick legs of an elephant denied this identity. Maybe there was still some respect for antiques, but it didn't include respect for people, to wit, the Peking dowager's tiny feet hugging mud-brick walls for support. Wasn't she was supposed to be carried?

Another off-limit tourist site was partly open for viewing. The famous Forbidden Palace had a roped balustrade, cutting off the rooms from entry but leaving an outdoor walkway for viewers. Elaborate silk tapestries, the velvet and satin of king and queen furnishings became a riot of color in Allie's head, trying to duplicate the forbidden camera. The gardens smelled of jasmine, rose, sweet alyssum, lotus fountains, peonies and always the huge odor-repellent mums, taking her back to high school football. Home sick? not quite, not yet, too busy agonizing for fireside comforts, too busy being a stand-in for Barney. Liaison officer, Nick Baker expressed surprise over Barney's bad luck, conveying official wishes for a fast recovery . . . The New York secretary, Mrs. Barker, had pressed her for a future shopping trip, explaining her hobby—collecting costumes from ancient dynasties. Although Allie preferred collecting old jade with its fading green and saving most of her allowance for art supplies, she recognized the urgency to have a shopping companion and nodded "yes." to Barker's invitation. She was learning the art of saving face, mulling over the Chinese: diulian, losing face, and its opposite, lianpi hou, having a thick skin. The business contract's face value demanded so much more thick skin than she or Barney had anticipated: they would skim the surface of everything like the Forbidden Palace with its untouchable secrecy. This memorial to ancient days lived up to its name as did the modern Friendship Store where its artifacts were fondled with ahs and ohs. With the next appropriate stop Allie purchased large sheets of rice paper, tapestry scrolls, and paper folding lanterns. An intricately carved sandalwood fan was a must-have because of its scrolling and pungent scent, and at least one silk folding fan or a non-folding fan, double layered with silk, scoped and braided with a handle of lacquered wood. A pair of golden tassels, French knotted, dangled down from the handle. One side displayed a pair of fan-tailed goldfish swimming below lotus pads. On the other side a butterfly pollinating an orange hibiscus, seemed headed for a cherry blossoms dangling overhead reminding of the sad Japanese story entitled <u>Madam Butterfly</u>: a suicidal Juliet with her Romeo not far behind.

Outside the store, fresh mountain air began its cooling trend. The scissors peak was photographed for future art as well as the tile-roofed post office that resembled an outdoor pavilion. The Summer Palace, equally ornate, stood forlorn, hiding its dynastic past while it belittled the flat roofs that made up suburbia. What an excellent subject Snap! Snap!

After walking many frigid steps, the wonton soup tasted very warming; it came with teriyaki, sub gum lo mein, and fried rice.

The small pagoda-restaurant on the Yangtze, normally closed, was opened for the special tourists who would take home glowing tales of Ch'in, the center of the world.

Leora's request for an outdoor market stop was grudgingly allowed with <u>fie dee</u>! hurry. All did a fast rummage through Chinese herbs, looking for beans long missing from their diet—pintos, limas, kidney or black beans.

"These beans no good for people . . . for cattle" the interpreter screwed up his nose and chuckled, but nothing else resembled a bean so Allie purchased a pound of what her compatriots labeled <u>Mung</u> beans.

From the open market, the minibus ignored the Forbidden City wheeling around the square to Tiananmen headed for the Hall of the People with a Museum of the Chinese Revolution.

Their counselor tour-guide announced, "Mao Zedong's life in special section We go there first. Please not use cameras." What a simple life! thought Allie, noticing the portrayal of every-day routine: a family gathering for a meal after working in the fields and orchards. Next came a display of outrageous abundance of commune products. Allie thought the posters and wall hangings to be gross exaggerations.

"Come over here," shouted Leora, "the barefoot doctor!" A rare ivory replica, dressed in a white uniform with a medical-bag shoulder backpack mounted on a bicycle.

"I think this is on the second page of the Lunar calendar they gave us. I have it book-marked for a reproduction. Hah! I may be over ambitious."

Separated from the pictorial life of Mao Zedong, the historical archives of dynasties began with Ch'in, 221 B.C. The first emperor, Shih Huang Ti, turned aristocracies into provinces and standardized character writing. Allie, a practiced skim reader, took a deep breath, and carried on. "Confucius influenced the next dynasty, the Han. Liu Pang. Though he was humble of birth, he seized all power and established Confucianism. Later, a more affluent dynasty, T'ang, established caravan routes" . . .

Leora yawned in boredom, but Allie stretched and excitedly read on.

"The Sung dynasty reorganized and Buddhism had a long peaceful reign until it lost out to religious persecution losing its monasteries and temples, Ah, here comes Genghis Kahn! Leora, wake up! have you seen the fabulous mannequin in Hong Kong? This Mogul warrior captured Peking in the north, then the south under the dynasty name, Yuan. They lasted almost one-hundred years until the Buddhist monk, Chu, established a new capital at

Nanjing. Civil government was reestablished. The Ming dynasty lasted a hundred years also. In 1644 the Manchu's were employed to help defend the Great Wall invasion by a Tung sic tribe. Then came deceit: the Manchu's took over for an 18th century high-point. So much for that century! The 19th brought a three-year opium war, thanks to Great Britain. Foreign bedfellows in general bypassed the great wall for trade, China's undoing, especially under the Dowager Empress, Tzu Hsi. Her retirement led to the Boxer revolt. Their secret society caused an anti-foreign revolt."

With hands on hips Allie had a sudden brainstorm. "These dynasties were about one-hundred years each. Max Heindel of the Rosicrucian Order says that astrological cycles correspond to human cycles. Pluto's revolutionary 100-year cycle coincides? Anyway, good old Chiang Kai shek tried to defeat communism but finally left the fighting up to Japan and the flying tigers in 1937. Barney and I met a couple of pilots in the Peking Hotel dining room whose fathers were <u>flying tigers</u> back then."

Being a few years older than Allie, Leora remembered communism's gain after World War II. "The People's Republic got underway using Marx-Lenin education. Familial piety went down the drain."

A shrill whistle sent them running to the minibus. And not too soon to avoid the sudden change of climate. Mongolian winds whipped across the tall mountains surrounding Peking. Allie's favorite, *scissors peak,* closed its gap, snipping off the sun, letting white knots of snow pass through to unblock old man winter.

The snow must have reminded Luke of their youngest specialist from New Hampshire. Only 18, a kid they loved and respected for his jovial outlook. "Has anyone been to visit Joey? He looks under the weather. Dysentery is getting the best of him."

Michael, the tornado victim, also known as Mitch, raised his hand, like a schoolboy. "He's no longer a clowning Heckle-Jeckle; he's become downright dangerous, dining alone with a scowl on his face, not speaking to anyone . . . he's like someone in a deep depression."

"I think his thermos water isn't being boiled long enough," suggested Leora, always Johnny on the spot.

"Or someone overlooked the process altogether," Luke's face looked drawn and wrinkled . . . it was his pensive pose.

Mitch explained his plan for a good deed, "I bought a Chinese yo-yo to make him laugh, if he'll just see me and share the joke, you know how the yo-yo rebounds and returns automatically. Maybe he will roll back to being the cool clown, or at least, civil." Mitch bounced with the bus and rolled his arms imitating the strange yo-yo's ability to return back once thrown out from the string.

"I have a good joke book," Popped up a newcomer, "but the British humor doesn't seem to phase Americans." Lester was a wiry Limey with a colloquial accent sitting next to Roger, a very sedate Londoner. The two chess experts had been around for a couple of weeks usually lounging in Han's room, but already had a Sunday habit of coming to Allie's painting area, her card table studio. She smiled remembering their fascination with her washouts of the background, then stroking a rose, petal by petal. It was a time that silence was therapeutic, the music exhilarating. Allie had spent hours at home recording from her FM radio, thinking ahead to playing tapes for just such an occasion. She could hear the music now as she reminisced.

Brilliant Roger loved both classical music and classical books. He was sorry he could not bring something Shakespearian to read defying the book burning . . . especially the classics. "Instead of Aesop's Fables, we're expected to enjoy <u>Quotations</u> <u>From Mao</u> <u>Zedong</u>."

Lester had added his two cents." Those rag-a-muffins could learn a lot more from Aesop than from Mao's Little Red Book. Even non-readers stash the red book in their boot-size pockets like wearing a fetish."

"Ma Le thinks a rebound is coming soon," Allie added "And by-the-way she was educated in England . . . she snatches everything I have to read including the Bible, not yet declared extinct. Something magic is still about, a residue of the old days, without kid-stealing and wife-beating. The people have been disciplined enough. Their unity does belong to the Cultural Revolution, but without more liberal schooling, democracy may never get to first base."

"Until the Red Guards out-grow their teen-age prankish," prompted Roger, "missing a childhood could rebound like . . . uh . . . yo-yo's."

"O Shangri Lai, come to me." moaned Lester's droll mockery.

"Better make it Bali Hai—with a bloody Mary. Ole to Les!" chortled Roger.

Les must have misheard the song on my tape recorder, Allie thought, having always kept it on when painting. As if someone had turned it off abruptly, she was jolted out of her reverie.

The minibus had plowed into a snow bank shocking the revelers into silence and neck grabbing.

When the vehicle had been pushed back onto the trail, mountains gave way to plains; occupants maintained their silent reverence until they sensed the nearness of the guest house. Wind and snow, dogging their path rapidly turned into sleet and ice. Leora reminded them of a welcome banquet for Lester and Roger, and yet-to-arrive, an American named Charlie Bishop, a Frenchman, Jacques, and a Hungarian, Gustav. Another Holland representative has a house to himself. He brought his wife and nine year old daughter. They're the Bogaards. They'll be sitting at the head of the table as guests of honor."

No one seemed to mind how Leora took over her husband's post, least of all, himself.

Just another anomaly, thought Allie, unusual, but not a dangerous border line.

Chapter 8

Christmas came softly with wreath and candle window decor, sharing rice paper, ribbon, and twine for wrapping a few packages to send home. Getting together to sing carols finds Allie poring over a lap violin with strings and buttons that look like typewriter keys. One hand strums while the other plays the key notes. She lets out a groan. "Its not like the lonely wail of the Erhu, not even the twang, but so much cheaper!" She snaps her fingers thinking of the agile hands with long nails playing the Erhu on the Saturday transition from political movies to real live musicals. Ah, what a wonderful transition that was from sitting in a cold, dark room of propaganda! The symphonic music was comparable to any she had ever heard and what a blessing for her ear-audits of the high sounds! While struggling over White Christmas, Roger must have been wincing his ears from a few doors down. He introduces Jacques, a tall bushy brows Frenchman dressed in black tweeds, a professional musician! Then whirls on his heels and scurries back to his chess game with Hans. A tournament is going on.

Jacques begins a sad melody from the movie production of Doctor Zhavago . . . somewhere my love there will be songs to sing . . . It seems amazing, she thought, how much melody he can eke out of a toy instrument. Then the sobbing begins.

"Oh, what is wrong? Your song is beautiful." She hands him a rare Kleenex from home, grateful that trees are still replanted in the U.S.

"It's about my lost love . . ." after dabbing his eyes and blowing his nose, he switches to a German folk tune . . . "you, you, you are my true love; you are my only love . . . ."

"You don't need to read notes like I do?"

"I played in a band before I joined the foreign job market."

Jacques reminded her of her college French professor, not only in his tall, dark stance, but in his outpouring of emotion, his deep baritone brogue.

Jacques eventually conducts a rousing medley of Christmas carols for the group of homesick expatriates.

Among the group sits a tall, business-like Hungarian with a goatee beard. Gustav reappears the following day having heard of her desire to sprout Mung beans. Being an expert in horticulture, he goes about the process of soaking and changing water every day or reminding Allie to do so, as his span is very short.

What delicious sprouts came from cattle beans! She sprinkled them over almost every side-dish brought to her place setting. The International Family was also sprouting in size and becoming closer knit until the Hong Kong food supply became a bone of contention, a grab bag of first come, first served. Who is hoarding cheese? Who got the canned ham? the sardines and crackers? or the peanut butter and crackers? Canned wieners, pineapple, coffee . . . ? The job site lingo sounded tame in comparison to the mud-slinging vindictive thrown about. No one knew exactly what food supplies were ordered. Was the Ugly American sprouting the fangs of a dragon?

Nevertheless, the Chinese did not gave up trying to please. After numerous banquets the dining room menu consisted of hundreds of dishes added on by request. Allie found an item that became quite popular, beginning with a big plate of noodles surrounded by numerous tiny bowls. Such delicacies brought everyone rushing to her table . . . she couldn't recall the item she ordered and neither could the houseboy. But what a one-time treat!

The banquet Leora had announced on the minibus came about on the western New Year of December 31st. The composite of troubled souls that Allie envisioned looked presentable, even Barney was able to attend. She had located the culprit and popped a bottle over him; from then on Chinese herbal soaking quickly shrank the swelling.

Joey, looking pale, pasted on a facial gesture between a grimace and a chortle. Lester and Roger appeared more lively, and for the sake of duty, performed gan bey!, bottoms up! Charlie, a middle aged specialist, slightly plump and bald, was the belle of the ball with his jovial banter, even his futility of trying to drink down the hosts. The Ugly American came to life slightly after midnight when all except Charlie had snuggled down to sleep.

Pounding on door after door, all suffered his booming voice, "Hey Joey come on out! Hey Jim, hey Nora, I'm so-ow wonesome . . . ." The aroused pair, Jim and Nora, had just arrived to begin their annual contract. They had been seated next to Charlie at the banquet table.

When the Smiths were paged, Barney nudged her to keep silent. "Let him rave; let his pounding fists murder us sleepers. The unit will complain." Hah! thought Allie, he must be suffering from a marital split.

The breakfast table became an altar for Charlie's repentance. From his name plate a tape recorder duplicated his booming voice Charlie turned purple with embarrassment, stammering his apologies, as well as confirming Allie's suspicions of losing a wife.

The recorder, Jim Ryan, was a muscular NFL star. His lithe, grinning wife, Nora, knew that he was also inclined to over-indulge and would be testing his ilk with Chinese tankards.

Nora reprimanded Charlie. "You had it coming! We lost a lot of sleep. I came from a medical family, nurse mother, doctor father. We relished our sleep."

Nora's medical background was helpful a short distance away from the guest house where the ladies had gathered to select some of the ripened grapefruit. An interpreter trainee was grasping to explain, "Your American, Loo-ees Burbank, bring us this fruit . . . show us how to grow for peasantry down south."

Nora intoned, "Its value is in the quinine that helps prevent malaria and hepatitis. I can imagine that the mosquito is rampant in the boggy rice swamps."

"We have priority before shipment." Leora tossed a fruit in the air and started filling her knapsack Allie was one again embarrassed by the grab bag approach.

Barney became her sounding board when he, arrived from work. With glinting eyes and hands on hips, she complained. "All of us are given shots of Gamma Globins as a general prophylactic. We could do without mountains of grapefruit stored in some of our rooms. Intended for the poor! Such greed!"

"Our theme song has to be 'live and let live.'" He wrapped the robe more tightly around his shivering torso . . . his shower had been agonizing in frigid water.

"The capitol of Hopei Province is where they say we are going tomorrow for a factory tour. I hope they make hot water heaters."

The compressor, instead, met with Barney's approval. "This is great for the plant. No more shoulder poles with buckets of water."

The long metallic building, dimly lit, required good eye sight for the manufacturing process. Compressors were proudly displayed for irrigating vegetarian produce, the way of life in this part of Hopei province.

Another building, almost dark, was a textile factory where women were tatting eyelet place mats, table cloths, fine bedspreads, and wall hangings. A wall size table cloth depicted a phoenix confronting an eagle. "What an appropriate display! The eagle is our symbol." Allie exclaimed to the group, not even considering a deeper meaning. All items were wrought in coarse cotton ecru.

This fetching tablecloth would commemorate my trip, she thought, noticing intricate eyelets plucked-out thread by thread, then over-cast by hand. She noticed colorful embroidery work on silk and satin wall tapestries, laboriously hand-stitched in dungeon light.

Allie asked the interpreter. "Could I have written permission to purchase cotton? Ten yards would be fine." She had been collecting material at home from dry-goods store sell-outs. These stores, individually owned, had seen their heyday.

She had purchased a new electric sewing machine to replace the inherited Singer pedal, the very machine they were using here. "I love to sew!" was a wasted remark on a Chinese clerk wearing government issue. Feeling sheepish about suffrage, she had asked Ma Li, "What do women dislike the most?"

"Cooking, <u>zao</u>, the kitchen stove," was the ready reply. No need to ask why, with wood and coal smoke permeating the air. A severe shortage of electricity prohibited better stoves, even if finances permitted.

The interpreter grasping the permission slip quickly disappeared into an office. Allie could hear "<u>dan wei</u>" but saw her pointing to the wall hanging.

The tea table ceremony was always the last event of the tour: Allie had made several purchases, but the most expensive, the beloved tablecloth, was actually given to her at the ceremony. What a precious gift, the phoenix and eagle! How she loved all that accompanied green tea! Not only the gift, but a permission slip, <u>dan wei</u>, to purchase cotton, U.S. cotton, in Peking.

The smell of textile and tea was soon replaced by pungent disinfectant a few kilometers later. The Peace Hospital, the brain child of Canadian Norman Bethune, had left a deep impression on Chinese culture. Bethune, like Burbank, brought his bag of tricks, his western medicine. A pillared rotunda with steps leading up to a central plaque, portrayed Bethune.

A glimpse in the open doors of the patient rooms emitted a potent smell of Lysol or a close equivalent, strong enough to anesthetize the whole hospital. Acupuncture demonstrations were given for every type of ailment, even surgery. It seemed incredible that needles in pressure points over the body could eliminate pain, as if telling the immunity system to get to work and heal this body!. Nora and Jim purchased take-home kits believing they could learn the technique. Bethune's western medicine was now so scarce that donations were more than welcome. Allie planned to leave behind medications she and Barney would have left over, vitamin pills, allergy medicine, aspirins, etc. She felt well inoculated with so many shots prior to embarking on this trip: typhus, diphtheria, smallpox, polio, and pneumonia headed the list.

The tea table at Bethune did not escape the disinfectant smell, but the pear-apple center piece was some help. English biscuits smelled cinnamon, going fine with green tea!

The tour ended with another beginning for Allie. Outside her door, a pair of despondent looking dark-skins were waiting for her return. "Habra usted Espanole?

High School Spanish had not been her cup of tea, but she recalled many nouns and some verbs. Pointing out objects around them, they soon had something going. She jotted down words and phrases until they could communicate. One Mexican knew no English or Chinese. The other, a roughish senior', with a small mustachio wore a glittering bull fighter vest and sombrero. He seemed very special to those who had worked with him elsewhere, passing by the open door and waving or pointing a finger up. He knew some English.

Allie was able to ask," Como si dice en Espanole?" pointing to something she couldn't remember in Spanish. Manuel would fill in the blank. She tried to warn of strong drink, as Molokai, for toasting, remembering how Mexicans loved to serve tequila to their shoppers.

They professed to enjoy keeping a rosy glow throughout the day, but tequila was like a soft drink in comparison.

No sooner had they arrived, than she was waving back and shouting adios to the smiling pair looking out the back window of the bus. Seating next to them was the well-dressed gentleman returning home from Mongolia. She hugged the serape around her shoulders, her gift from Manuel, glad to have been helpful in both cases.

Chapter 9

Success tugged at her ego; she wondered about counseling with Hans. He was going shopping again. This time Allie decided to accept the invitation since Jacques was also on board. She was interested in Chinese toys and wasn't disappointed in the wide range of exotic choices. The guides vacated the store very rapidly so they could shop unimpeded. The prying eyes incessantly stared through windows, cracks, and doors, one especially she nick-named snake eyes.

Jacques, being used to an audience, treated them all upon leaving. What a memoir to take home! the large circle with Jacques in the middle playing one of her toy harmonicas, shaped like a dragon. Such melodious music from a toy! Sayonara . . . The Flower Drum Song, and Alloueta had everyone clapping hands. She wouldn't let the bushy-haired moocher bother her; he seemed to be always hanging around whenever she was out in public. His eyes were as beady as a cobra's, as slanted as a bowie knife.

Back at the Guest House another short-term specialists had arrived with his wife and teen-aged school drop-out. Their son,

Donald, wanted Allie to describe the Chinese New Year—the last excursion they had just missed.

His parents, Matt and Vivian sat protectively on each side of him as Allie explained the Gregorian calendar's lunar cycles. "We knew it was the year of the dragon and weren't sure of where we were headed, but silence didn't last very long. Imagine looking down from a hotel balcony encased in glass and seeing a million people! standing in absolute silence until the fireworks began, then they let loose shouting and singing. What lovely sparkles! their own invention on display in the sky, ending with Moa Zedong's portrait and a red star."

"Where did so many people come from? The teenager inquired.

"Mostly communes. In trucks or in donkey-drawn wagons. I've never seen so many at once and so orderly. In the states there would have been a big clean-up of popsicle sticks and gum wrappers, firecrackers, and roman candles."

Don smiled and nodded in agreement, looking out the window wistfully at the white snow. His father, Matt, responded with a suggestion. "We've never seen such a sight. How about a snowball war?"

Jumping into coats, scarves, and gloves, their cowboy boots made swift tracks. Not only gathering snow, but onlookers who decided to join the fun. Joey, bent on ice carving and Lester and

79

Roger ringing out with the Volga boatman song: their ho heave ho ended with roll, roll, roll your snow or merrily, merrily, merrily, life is but a dream.

They were working on the belly bottom while Mark helped Don and Matt roll and pack enough snow for the head. Hans showed up with a hilarious coolie hat. Jacques had a drum stick with a French flour de lieu for the snowman to hold. Don slipped a tiny American flag into the straw tent-like hat. His mother, Vivian, had come running outdoors to supervise her flag donation, a dinner-favor from her Health Club. Her send-off had occurred on President's Day.

The three ladies, Allie, Leora, and Nora, were invited to a tea at the Bogaards to welcome Vivian on board, especially since she was into yoga, encouraging all to exercise. "Nah, said plump Leora, "we do a lot of walking around the premises, playing table tennis and throwing quoits and basketball."

"And don't forget the sight seeing tours; they walk our legs off!" added Nora.

"I'm the sitting bull," admitted Allie, "I like to paint and do so every minute I can, but I felt downright ornery in the recreation room when I had to have a chair to eat sitting down. I needed my lap at least to balance the snack plate while the Chinese were standing up eating like acrobats. A Chinese style cafeteria, <u>Yum Cha</u>."

"That was the New Year featuring food specialties. They served noodles with sea food and sesame balls for desert. They gave us chairs too." Leora pointed to Nora.

Newcomer Vivian was also on to cooking skills proving useful after a spring commune visit. The weather had finally turned balmy and fruit was being harvested. Vivian sat stiffly, yogi posture-conscious, with her husband, Matt and son, Don. The Mueller's, and Smiths had on sweaters, shivering but paying attention to the translated lecture on commune life: the pigs could not climb up hill out of their dugouts, fruit was preserved by underground storage. Even the carved banquet ice had originated in underground caverns.

"Old eggs? A year old? Ugh!" Don was shushed up by his father. Baskets of apples, pears, and pear-apples were donated as gifts. The communists claimed to have grafted the pear-apple. But Allie believed Burbank had developed this at the Institute where they were given grapefruit.

Back at the guest house Vivian declared her intentions. "Hey gals, let's make some apple pies, the old American standby."

Leora confessed to hoarding. "I . . . uh . . . have a box of biscuit dough, and some margarine." Nora admitted to a jar of honey. So they were off and running or rather peeling fruit with the Chinese chef's promise to bake their pies in one of their huge iron ovens.

Allie saw a chance to take her leave, "Bye, bye girls, I'm off to paint; apple pie's not my cup 'o tea." She admitted to liking fresh apples but now she hungered to paint some of the sketches wasting away on the sketch pad. She had snapshots of Jonquil and tulips fields taken in Holland, wishing a windmill could be included . . . She had asked Hans for a picture, and he thought he had one on a calendar. Like a bolt of deft blue, she recalled his open invitation. After dinner she followed up on it.

"Tonight is poker night for Barney, so I thought it would be a good time to accept your Thanksgiving invite. I'd like to hear some of your tapes and oh, did you come up with a windmill?"

"Sure, sure, come on in; I'll put on the recorder." He chose dinner music, then soft rock. He ripped a page from his calendar, regarding her along with a yearning come-dance-with-me look. How she longed to melt into his arms and forget her vows of chastity! She knew that would be foolish . . . shades of Leora who had spent the night with him after a drinking bout, coming by the next morning looking very pale and shameful for what she had done. Allie wanted to shake some sense into her, turning up her nose at the stale liquor smell.

After an hour of listening to the musical variety, Hans remarked, "Well that's I have unless you want to spend the night?"

Ignoring his invitation, she snuggled into her Mexican Poncho, thanked him for the windmill picture and departed. <u>Gracias y adios</u>.

Grateful for solitude at her card table drawing board, she sketched the windmill, then dabbed fields of yellow bulbs around the canal. Next, she turned her attention to watercolor roses. Lester had requested a valentine for his wife.

Chapter 10

A ship this size had never been tackled by the Smiths; they were used to small fishing skiffs, not a rope ladder obstacle course Allie missed Barney's brawn to lean on, but he had already adroitly climbed the rope rungs ahead of her. The tight fitting navy blue pant suit was stretched to the limit. Loafers kept searching for toeholds, but finally she reached the top rung where Barney and Luke's hands reached out. They both saluted, "Quartermasters on duty! Welcome aboard."

Despite the supply ship's size, Allie felt claustrophobic looking into the dinky state rooms with saucer-size portholes. Snapping her fingers, she made a quick comparison with the excruciating air flight and painful ears. "Barney can we go home by ship?"

"I'm afraid not; air fare is already pre-paid, but we could take Japan Air to the states."

"Hey guys!" shouted Luke, "Let's go to lunch, then look around the town. We know Tientsin's history;" winking, he added, "but not its character."

Lunch at the Seaman's Club topped all dinners since their arrival. Won-ton sour hot soup, stuffed dumplings, egg rolls, and

Peking duck. An almond cookie accompanied smooth tasting green tea. She was all smiles stepping down from the three-story clubhouse. A warmth from the Yangtze held back sleet and snow. The Chinese driver gesticulated widely explaining how the city had been quartered off by foreigners. A secret society—the Boxers caused an anti-foreign uprising in 1900. His swinging arms and word by word description was fraught with emotion, rarely shown by Chinese inscrutability. It was as if he personally recalled the tragic war to expel foreigners. Their ghosts crying out to beware of such as they! Was the speaker being derogatory? The divisional lines were still apparent in the ruins; the scars were not completely healed?

Allie wanted to add: western trade, Sun Yat-sen, education, and now us but thought better of it, their down play had been reflected in a mirror of frowns, grimaces, groans . . . change!

The Old City's crumbled bricks and stones were again on fire, ignited by a colorful sunset along with fishermen and women around the jetties. A flat-bottom sampan featured a well-respected fishing-cormorant, its raison de affairs for being kept alive and well. The incredible junks with high sails glowed in the sunset. The stars did not glitter until the official car pulled up in the circular drive. The travelers were more than anxious for a restful night, thinking of tomorrow's Sunday birthday party. Nora was having her 25th birthday and Jim wanted to do something special. His recording of Charlie's atrocious drunken brawl blamed on his impending divorce may have been therapeutic for the group in general. Jim was a doting husband and wanted to do something quite the opposite for Nora. His note to Leora requested a birthday cake. On a separate note for the cook, he penned, "write happy birthday Nora, with icing."

Most were invited to visit Nora and share her cake. Guest house occupants trickled in one by one. Gifts were mostly wrapped in rice paper. Chinese Checkers purchased in the Guest House store were from Joey. He had recovered from his despondency, refusing to drink water, boiled or not. He would survive on sodas and whatever juice was available.

With a flamboyant courtesy, Hans proffered a tin of Gouda cheese. "Best wishes to a cheese-y lady."

Charlie's bottle of champagne made a loud pop when uncorked. He dutifully poured a drink in a paper cup from the expatriate kitchen. "May you stay forever young . . . beautiful . . . and married.!"

A folding fan and lantern from Lester and Roger respectively caused a pang of homesickness for Allie. Pageantry fanfare, a folding lantern with a candle, took her all the way back to elementary school. She loved imitating an oriental dancer, swinging her fans and strings of lotus blooms, or looking for "made in China" on every toy.

Vivian, well-known for her latticed apple pies, continued to be resourceful. She had dipped a perfect rose in hot wax after getting official permission to pick her choice of a scarlet attar. Melting a white candle with her husband's cigarette lighter was clever.

Oh well, thought Allie, my watercolor rendition will be ready to frame. She can take it home protectively rolled up.

Jacques played <u>Happy Birthday</u> on Allie's lap violin while Leora ushered in the cake from the Chinese kitchen. The icing oozed over with its verbatim message: <u>write happy birthday Nora with icing</u>. "Very funny McGee," scowled Jim.

"Very Chinese-y," chortled Jacques.

The aloof Bogaards in their old-fashioned homestead of a house entered the social circle by way of sour kraut. With so much cabbage on hand, Vivian had asked in vain for sour kraut. When Edda Bogaards got wind of this, she invited the ladies to use her kitchen to shred and soak the cabbage. "I have an old time recipe: you soak for nine days, rinse and pack in jars. It was popular in Rotterdam during World War II and is still used today . . . " Her voice was squeezed and high, her form short and plump. The ladies debated, combining their knowledge of this culinary art, making some compromises, and using a contrivance that resembled a paper cutter. They finally made some neat shredding. Cabbage and salt were dumped into a big old fashioned wash tub. Spices added later.

While observantly cooling her heels, Allie inquired about Victoria's schooling. "A nine-day kraut for a nine-year old; she will love it! . . . oh, I teach her myself using the international at-home system. The Chinese take it all in; call it envy! "Madonna an' girlie ve–ly close."

The next cabbage of any note was part of a centerpiece on the Welcome to Spring banquet table. It was their recreation room where carrots, radishes and turnips carved into flowers—roses, mums, and daisies augmenting the ice dragon to welcome spring. The friendly Bignonia dragon was thought to inspire new life, new crops, and propagation of animals. Humans, already overabundant, must be excused from Bignonias' blessing. Water lilies floated on pads; a turnip-orchid graced a lettuce bog. Cabbage bowls supported carrot rosebuds.

Place mats were huge leaves resembling elephant ear, lotus or, thought Allie, Grandma's wild poke weed so delicious when boiled with salt pork, but never topped with chiao-tzu, the Chinese dumpling. Chop sticks clicked in rapid staccato. Bamboo bowls of noodles and fried rice were topped with sauces and soups passed from hand to hand, course after course.

Rice wine toasts seemed endless, honoring the success of the commune; grain production being up 52% within ten years. They toasted the plant construction with new farming implements; restoring of irrigation; (surface wells had become dry.) Rain known as sky water was scarce; the electrified wells 30-50 meters deep, made up for the drought. The last toast became unfortunate for those who lost control. Jim slipped on the stairs en route to the ping pong balcony. The next morning his leg was double its normal size, in fact, so badly broken that he could not work for the remainder of his job fulfillment. Allie shook her head sadly, thinking how close she came to breaking a leg climbing the rope ladder.

"Well, Charlie's had his revenge without lifting a finger!" He growled, thinking he had it coming!

Doctors arrived in groups, shaking their heads. Finally, they sent him to Hong Kong. That, too, was hopeless. The surgery needed was beyond their scope. He would have to be operated on in the states as soon as he returned home, and that wouldn't be until the contract date ended.

Nora's Yahztee game was played continuously. The dice could be heard jingling down the hall, a game being played to help Jim stay immobile with a cast until dismissal date. His strength and normal good health would be something to fall back on. The door stayed open for visitors, hopefully with cheerful attitudes. Joey and Mitch often came to joke about the mishaps on the job site.

"Teaching scholars to manipulate machines is hilarious! Female welders—hah, hah" exploded Joey.

"Stateside, this plant would already be built," commented Mitch. "And I'd be there when the baby comes."

"And, I could drink some damn good water!" added Joey.

"Say, how is the water in Hong Kong? We have an R&R coming up." Mitch winked at Joey, "I'll bet you would like to borrow Hans' little black book.

Barney and Allie had taken a folding chair and guffawed with the jokers pulling for Jim. I think we'll stay in China," Barney commented, with a lingering look at Allie. "I missed out when my leg was swollen, and since Allie didn't see the Great Wall or Peking Zoo, we can check out the Pandas and doesn't the Embassy have Coca Colas?"

How could she resist this itinerary! "Sure, we could take in Hong Kong some other time. Going home would take too much travel time."

Allie waved her arms and shook her amber curls, remembering Leora's comment: if you don't mind cold water, they do a great job of washing and setting. This meant that the French were still around and her hair had grown like wild and so had Barney's. "Peking here we come!"

Chapter 11

Once the Tourist Bureau got wind of the Smith's intentions, flattered that they chose to spend their R&R in China, they went to work on a whirlwind agenda. And soon, a guest house driver helped them get settled on the Peking Express with two small bags and a folded tote. They were escorted to a dining room all to themselves. A moment later they were wishing they'd had the driver help them with an order. Trying pantomime, Barney wound up flapping his arms and crowing like a rooster. The waiter nodded and whisked away returning shortly with the biggest platter of scrambled eggs they had ever seen.

"At least, we'll get enough sulfur to last us for quite some time."

"Nourishment with great taste; have a home-made roll." Allie passed a covered basket.

Peking streets were crowded as usual with people, bicycles, three-wheeled vehicles and a few small cars. Allie was amazed to see two black ladies wearing designer clothes descending the steps of the Peking Hotel. The new business immigration, the leap forward movement; youthful and well-proportioned, what beauties! She wondered which province of Africa they hailed from. Their small hats resembled Spanish mantillas. Their faces were small and symmetric, the first blacks she had seen on this side of the world.

They slid past the ladies who were making a slow decent in spike heeled pumps. Allie wondered if they had been banqueting, caught in dining room bartering for some enterprise.

The Liaison office, established only three years previously, was a result of President Nixon's visit. Barney still hedged away from embassy politics. Good by to Coca Cola for now. The only machine in China was located at the American embassy. So instead of reaching into her handbag for a coin to purchase a Coke, she accidentally touched her ballpoint. No longer taunted by hotel stationery, she would write her family before any more globe-trotting. Sandy had always been a doting sister; it was time for her to return the solicitation. Flopping into a hotel bamboo chair, she began:

Dear Sister,

You wouldn't believe the good and bad Barney and I have already met with in the People's Republic. In small, sly ways, the pendulum is trying to swing back to the old days before Mao's Cultural Revolution.

The people want less shuffling around with their job talents. How can a born school teacher become a welder or a hog butcher, or a trained secretary become a telephone lineman? It's been going on for over thirty years. They will never starve so long as they can grow rice and cabbage and peanuts galore. If I ask a Chinese lady what she dislikes the most. It is always cooking. And no wonder! she is confined to a coal burning cook stove like our great-grandmas used. The air is filled with smoke. I feel that I have time-traveled into the past century. Barney and I keep ducking the strong liquor they drink for toasting. How they survive it is a miracle. Our team is either having bad accidents or giving in to the curse of addiction.

The water cannot be boiled long enough for some of us. Barney and I are the only ones who haven't had dysentery, thanks to the halizone I had some trouble purchasing before we left. It meant talking a druggist into an ill-advised purchase. He relented only after I explained my raison d'affaires.

My widow's peak is still gray, but the curls are Mae Murray, thanks to the permanent wave from a time-vented machine brought here from Hong Kong. Leora, the site rep's wife, knows how to get anything she wants, but she wouldn't suffer a permanent wave after it arrived. Oh yes, I have an appointment with a French coiffure stylist here in Peking. They obviously didn't leave with the Boxers.

Easter is coming up. I will celebrate by purchasing a porcelain egg or some lacquer ware.

Please give my love to Mom and Dad, and you take care. I am not sure this will get to you. Everything is censored.

Your loving sister, Allie

P.S. Save me a Coca Cola!

The post office was a red pagoda surrounded by the typical portico with its tile roof curving upward. The steeple-shaped top marked it as an evacuated Buddhist haven. A table tennis game was in progress when she entered. She greeted them with hello in pinyin, "zhong wen," holding out the letter she added, "bao zhong," take care of this. The letter was weighed; an abacus decided the postage, but not its true destiny.

When the cold water doused her scalp Allie hollered, "Ouch! Bu hao," bad, or not good, was met with dur bu chi!, excuse me! She was under the thumb of a strong handed hair washer, "cold water for washing; heated water for rinse."

The French stylist said her folks came here from Cannes where she had learned how to design the uplifted style a regal fanfare that Allie loved. She remembered to say tai miei le, how beautiful! tipping one yuan, grinning to think of one-seventh of a U.S. dollar. She surmised that the process as a whole was worth the long wait sitting in a row of women shifting around on cold metal chairs.

Barney's hair, on the other hand, looked like a cockle burr. She could see that he didn't want another hair cut until landing on U.S. soil. How would Hans regard him?

The R&R was a horizontal vanishing point. Something was planned for every day. Though drivers wheeled them about, their walking shoes were invaluable, especially for the Great Wall. After the first flight of steep brick steps, Allie became breathless. She leaned on the tour guide and rested against one of the parapet windows. The guide comforted her by saying, "This is as far as Nixon could walk."

Under the archway Allie's panoramic view was so awe-inspiring she could not imagine it a killing field with arrows defending their protective wall from invaders. Mountains as well as brick and mortar hid fertile valleys and gardens. She felt so calm she hated to leave this peaceful terrain, but Barney was waiting in the car. Later she'd mull over the desperation for trade that finally made a notch in the wall though it lasted only a few years.

Their tour guide she had leaned against earlier measured only about five feet with crow black hair and bangs. Seeming well-informed, she cited, "The wall began its existence during the Ch'in dynasty 221 BC. It's now about 1500 miles long, 25 feet high and 15-30 feet thick at the base. It tapers to 12 feet. Watchtowers are up to 40 feet high."

"Didn't we climb the inner wall that surrounds the old city?" asked Allie.

"Yes, it runs south from Peking to Handan."

Barney suddenly pointed out the window, "Those huge marble sculptors look like lions, now I see an elephant, a camel, and there's a horse! Why are they beside the road?"

"Guarding the emperors' tombs—Ming dynasty's Avenue of Animals."

Other avenues awaited needing more shoe leather. The Zoo was too expansive to tackle in one outing. Barney felt relieved that the pandas were close to the entrance as he exclaimed, "Here come our cherished teddy bears walking like penguins!"

The pandas lumbered to piles of stalks, rolling into balls, chewing, and rolling like endless whirligigs. "How bamboo does grow! just like the saplings I planted on grandpa's farm. Within a few years a bamboo grove buffered his pond from north winds."

"Too bad we can't import a Panda . . . odd that bamboo can grow anywhere, but Pandas belonged to a vanishing forest, a remnant of old Ch'in. Their designated lunch stop beckoned them from across the street, elegant and spacious. They exchanged greetings with a slick-haired white-coat, surprising them with slurred English.

"Halloo, ni hao. Howe you like-e zoo?"

"Ho, good! she responded, much larger than Tsangchow's zoo, monkeys roam out of cages there." She gave Barney a sidelong glance, not having told him about her trip with Hans to a small out-of-the-way zoo. Needing Hans as an escort, she was fearful of the snake-eyed stalker who seemed to be aware of every outing.

She stared overhead at the Russian chandelier, then pointed to a cozy fireplace. They had been told by the tour guide that this restaurant had been closed to the public since severing relations with Russia.

"Soviets invaded Czechoslovakia,." the guide had explained, knotting her red scarf. "They attacked border guards in Manchuria in 1969. It is now forbidden to utter the word, Russia; so the agency decided to open their dining room just for you."

It was the same old routine as the guest house except Vodka replaced Molokai. "Vodka, re-al vodka, velly rare!"

They covered their stem ware with their hands. "No, no vodka, thank you."

A live duck was brought in for their approval, "No, please, no!. Bu hao, excuse, zar jian," waving a symbolic good bye and hollering, "let it go!"

Some Cantonese dishes were finally brought in. "Hmm . . ." cried Barney, "delicious noodles and fried rice; but no thanks to mushrooms; they taste like rubber bands . . . a relative of Portobello?—still no thanks. Please pass the stuffed dumplings."

Fried won tons, crab Rangoon, Szechuan stir fries, egg foo young–the dishes were endless. Carbonated soda, always present, replaced H2O. Thank you Lord for your guidance and protection.

After lunch, their Great Wall guide rejoined them, explaining how walls became more protective than fences. Bridges also formed dividing lines as Allie soon learned while walking to the center of such a divider to get a closer view and take a picture of the floating lilies. The guide frantically waved her arms, warning her to go no farther. The Red Guard standing at the far end had cocked his rifle. Whew! how many more narrow escapes, she wondered, scampering back the way she came.

Thirty-five foot walls surrounded the Forbidden City's palace grounds protecting former dynasties. The raven-haired guide now had a face that resembled a squeezed lemon as she motioned them to go inside the ancient Ming tomb; she would wait outside. Her waiting became understandable when acrid air hit their nostrils. Layers of dust permeating archives around jade and lacquer artifacts, silk hangings yellowed with age. The double line was suddenly broken by a terrified mother holding an infant close to her bosom. One look at Allie's strange vermillion face was a bad omen, the curse of a foreign devil! She quickly covered the tiny face with its blanket and dashed for the entrance leaving the superstition still dangling from tattered pages of history novels. The omen of bumping into a foreigner proved benefic for Allie when floundering around with and an errant dialect in the Friendship Store. She had left Barney at the hotel to rest while she used her cotton-permission slip, intending to purchase silk for painting a wall hanging. Traipsing the aisles of the Friendship Store, she thought she had memorized the phrase for silk, but much to her consternation she was taken to the toilet—a dialect problem. The omen-foreigner appeared, but looked quite Aryan, a thin apparition towering over squat yellow skins, she was cantering along, passing around slow amblers when Allie almost tripped her, crying out in a panic, "Do you speak English?"

"Why yes. I'm Nan Wells. I work for the International Relations Agency. ""Oh, could you help me? I'm trying to purchase a yard of silk . . . just to hone my painting skills. My dialect seems to be a tad off. My name is Allie Smith from the U.S."

Nan summoned a clerk and rattled off Chinese as if she were born there then quickly left. This no-nonsense business woman obviously had her contract to fulfill, but left Allie wondering about Nan's native soil.

Not only was the stiff white silk purchased, but ten yards of white nainsook cotton when she handed over her permission slip. Now happy to return to the job site armed with a new hobby layout to eventually pack away for her U.S. home studio.

They sauntered lazily into an empty dining room, being the first back from their R&R.

Barney noticed a white coat stacking up chairs to exchange a light bulb. From back to seat, seat to back, chair after chair, up, up to a lofty ceiling. He began designing a ladder, sketching it out on a paper napkin. The ladder was a new invention as none were seen on the job site or elsewhere. The ladder would soon became a reality with their hosts expressing great gratitude. <u>Duo xie ni,</u> thank you very much. No longer was the most agile employee to mount shaky chairs.

Barney's good deed brought back her vision. She felt that God had told her to go about the Guest House doing good It was during a gathering of the staff and expatriates, a social gathering to discuss the work progress. Her head began to nod; she said a silent payer for guidance. Then a vision of God appeared—a distance apparition, sitting on a chair telling her to go about the guest house doing for others. From that moment on she racked her brain for ways to be of help. Some paintings, framed or unframed, could be left behind. Like Bethune and Pasteur she now had a bag of tricks.

Chapter 12

The dining room was unusually quiet as if all were still savoring their exotic two-week respites with succinct food and wine. Then everyone tried to speak at once. A bedlam of noisy exchanges, welcomes, and what happened to you? Where did you go? Let's hear your tale of adventure. Chaucer couldn't have penned more variety or vanity.

Hans approached the Smith table. "Well, who have we here? Josephine and the Bald Eagle! Welcome back from History. How was the big city?"

"Very enlightening, thank you. I let Allie do the walking to save on my leg, still a little sore, thanks to the fiddler."

"Ah, smart choice. No wonder her legs are you know . . ." He hand-shaped and guffawed."

"Oh, we did have a few scrapes," intoned Allie. "I was the bad dragon to a terrified peasant, thinking I was putting a curse on her infant—an evil eye! She thrust the blanket over its face and fled. I felt like a worm, wishing I could crawl out of the tomb, far away from Ming dynasty superstitions. His lordship wouldn't miss me a bit."

"Oh, yes he would. Hang in there. Welcome back!"

Her legs seemed to be trembling. Maybe she had done too much walking or was overexcited by the ribald exchange.

The Smiths were both surprised by how radiant Luke and Leora were after basking in Hong Kong sunshine, having visited Tiger Balm Gardens, a photographer's paradise, then Sung Dynasty's village and wax museum. How excited these old travelers became as they articulated. "Genghis Kahn does look ready to ride away for another excursion across Asia and Europe and on beyond. Thanks, Allie, for reminding me to look him up." Leora remembered being prompted at the Museum of History.

"And don't forget the acrobats" sighed Luke, "brandishing their swords, quite dangerously: the mock wedding's an on-going tribute. I think this dynasty goes back a thousand years, but lives on with great fanfare! My thanks, Allie, for a pushing us in the right direction."

'Coming back through Peking, we shook hands with Ambassador George Bush and his wife, Barbara . . . just to let them know we were managing one of the eight urea plants under contract, thanks to the new open door."

Facing Barney, he stressed his words, "you should go by the home office on your next trip to Peking."

Barney shook his head, "They don't guarantee us safe conduct. I'm reminded of the Levy's, our next-door neighbors. They were murdered . . . not because he was a new union boss from New York City, but because he and his small son were over-trusting Jews, lending their gun to a teenager who turned it on them."

Allie finished his story. "Stalkers could have the same feelings toward us as the country bumpkin had toward the Levy's. I have an eerie feeling sometimes of being stalked. Father and son were traipsing in the shooter's territory where he was likely to do his snipe hunting. No doubt he grew up hating Jews. Wrong place, wrong time for the innocent pair. My snake-eyed culprit may be an over-active imagination cropping up wherever I go without a tour guide." The Moeller's were staring, speechless as Allie continued. "Other neighbors and I took food casseroles to Mrs. Levy and her daughter. The widow was out of control, trying to wash away her loss by indulging in wine."

Finally, Luke spoke pleadingly to the group as a whole when the staff was out of ear-shot. "I know we are being shuffled about secretly in and out of places and vehicles like hostages, but the last quarter of the contract is coming up, so let's try to bear up without any more accidents! Please!"

May Day festivities seemed safe enough. Children's Day. Their overnight tour had a hotel reservation in Shijiazhuang, the capitol of Hopei province. Leora announced, "Qing Ming, means welcome to spring. Sweep the graves, light the candles, fly the kites, have a picnic . . . or join a parade—we've been invited to join The March of the Dragon."

Following a huge bass drum and crash cymbals with deaf-wrenching bongs, Allie's ears began to ring unmercifully. She tottered off-balance, crumpling beneath a eucalyptus tree. Snake eyes was waiting where the stalking was easy. "<u>Um ho gow gee aw!</u>, stop bothering me!" He prodded her with a drum stick. "<u>Jaaw hoy!</u>, Go away!" She cried. Being startled and frantic, she sat up quickly and was half off and running but not quickly enough. Down came the stick with a vicious blow across the back. One blow would not appease his anger. As he raised his weapon for a second strike, he was knocked aside by strong arms on both sides. Barney and Hans had pounced out of their parade line and used a hammer-lock to drag him away. Guest House officials, never far from their charges, took over from there.

"Whew! What a close call! Are you still in one piece?"

"I . . . I think so, Hans . . . Thank you for h-helping Barney."

"Yeah, it took two of us, said Barney. He was out to kill. Want to go back to the hotel?"

"No, no, I'd like to see the per-performance. He knocked the devil out of my ears . . . we—we're supposed to welcome dragon—harbinger . . . of change. At least, the snaky stalker's g-gone. My head is clearing."

The tragedy is over, she thought, my private show must go on, knowing her assailant would be expected to apologize profusely if he were to stay free. As wards of the State, the entrepreneurs commanded legal protection. She vowed to be more careful in the future resolving the ugly American stigma, instead of dramatizing one. She had fallen at home after surgery. It was nothing new; the middle ear controlled balance. She'd buy a nice cane like the one she saw the lily-foot woman leaning on. It could also serve as a weapon if need be.

The audience seated across the river from the performance included the intractable Allie with her soft drink and aspirin donation by the staff, and the guest house hospitality chairman had slipped her a ginseng pill. They obviously admired her bravado.

The stage was an outdoor theater set up across the narrow river inlet. A giant urn of peonies stood sentinel on each side while flags waved over the flat theater roof. A live swan trio: cob, pen and cygnet, floating gingerly around pads of lotus, separated the performers from their exuberant audience. But the audience was close enough to absorb and empathize with the melodious lute-family instruments, as well as agile performers. The pipa, sheng, yueqin, erhu, glockenspiel, and the Chinese wood block resounded like gentle winds. A gong stood suspended at the ready with a mat in hand. Although the orchestra was wearing government navy blue, one musician was sporting a skirt, balancing a cello between her legs. Also defiant were bongo drummers, Qin strummers, and Slun minority choirs wearing rainbow robes with beadwork and braids using this special occasion to oppose the dress code.

Willow trees offered sparse shade. Sweating African drummers vanished off stage to make room for bamboo-limber acrobats to execute their balancing acts with yo-yo, chair and swing. Tight-rope walkers holding parasols evoked gasps and loud applause. Snare drums maintained a low drum beat, as low as a funeral dirge. Allie recalled the Peking Opera she had attended at her university alumnus. Having always asked for a block of complimentary tickets, she invited everyone she knew to The Circle of Chalk where performers used meager stage props: a chair could become a mountain, a tree or a throne. Hand fluttering could be a stream of water, and the versatile fan expressed various emotions, depending on how fast or slow it waved and to whom it pointed when folded. No real stage props were needed as the audience became engrossed, letting the plot unravel imaginations. Batons could be violin bows for courting or swords for slaying the dragon.

She winced with pain, sipping her soda: she had become the victim of the baton holder's hatred, playing the unintended part of a foreign devil. The low drum beat made her want to sob, but acrobatic dancers held her in sway with leap-turns, jazz-splits, and swastika-poses. They were ousted by the dragon, then on comes the traditional Lion Dance: an oversize head of paper mache` with macramé` fringes hanging down, heavy haired mane, tasseled teeth Under the long silk body the tail dancer followed the head dancer while staying attuned to the drum beat until . . . at last, disrobing for applause. Their eyes no longer looked slanted but wide with excitement.

"Are your eyes still slanted?" came a startling question from her sub-conscience. Equally startling was the phone call from a childhood neighbor. She only remembered the name because it was so unusual. Seibenhausen.

"What a surprise! Heavens no, it must have been the Dallas sun or the hail that peppered our house scaring me out of my sight!" Allie shook off her reverie when the beat changed with everyone singing . . . "the East is red . . ."

For once she wished her eyes had been slanted enough to thwart the blow. Her attacker's cry was a trumpet blast, "Jian die, jian die! Bourgeois jian die!" Spy, spy, bourgeois spy! more vile than the ringing in her ears, upsetting her balance, as she tried to crawl under a bush.

She wanted to face snake eyes with gai si! go to hell! answering back with job site slang, but the surprise attack rendered her helpless; her only defense was rescue, prayer . . . Almighty God, send angels! Now! Please! Was it the cry of the attacker or the caw of a crow that alerted her to sit up, avoiding a second blow to the head?

Helpful hands ignored the "don't touch" rule as they escorted Allie on her personal Long March back to Hotel Shijiazhuang. Luke was waiting; she had to face his ack, ack prior to sinking into the herbal admixture and hope for warm water. Leora could be very helpful making arrangements. The medley of herbs would relieve the back ache and soothe ruffled feathers once she got used to the wild, weed-like stink. The crow could have been a rare escapee from the bird-eaters or another clairvoyant vision. She hummed a tune she remembered from elementary school.

Jasmine stars on the green, green spray

Bloomed for the birds at the dawn of the day.

Before returning to Tsangchow, the culprit who lacerated her back was dragged to her room to apologize or be executed. He professed his sorrow. "<u>Bu hao Yi si dur bu Qi</u>," promising to observe future politeness, <u>ming tian</u>, to foreigners as indicated by the Communist Manifesto. His sentence was an out-house clearing job for a period of two years. <u>Laodong gaizao,</u> laboring as a form of rehabilitation. The stink would be enough to banish any errant thoughts of future violence. Just walking past an out-house or urine factory was sickening to the olfactory sense. Barney's urea plant would be a great innovation. And so would the healing herbs be Allie's innovation to cure the sorely bruised shoulder-to-back wound.

Chapter 13

Although spare time was limited to only one day per week, the hard-working expatriates spent some free time comparing short-wave radios and exchanging news bits. The best time for clearest communication with The Voice of America, BBC, Tokyo news, or Hong Kong? The broadcasts were their only contacts with world-wide news. Television and computers, alien to this part of the world, were toys left behind to be appreciated upon arrival home. They were two hours by rail, south of Peking's pair of acceptable hotels and an embassy's passing acquaintance.

Winter's cold melted into June's unusual coolness. Work delays could now be caught up.

Toward the end of the month plans were made to celebrate U.S. Independence Day. This year, 1976, was America's centennial year . . . Fireworks, yan huo, were easily ordered, a specialty going back to the original hand grenade, tetra howl, protecting the great wall and even rocketing between ships at sea.

Their Chinese hosts were asked about building a ramp for launching rockets. A dian, pad for launching fireworks, yan huo, fa she. This brought gales of guffaw—not a surprise, considering the Chinese New Year celebration. The well-mannered crowd had cleared an area for the bravados holding fireworks in shaky hands until at the last minute releasing them into the night sky with never a mishap. After all, they did invent the dangerous but beautiful art. A ramp? Ha, ha. They'd have to build their own!

Costume planning was left to the ladies. Vivian proved to sew a mean seam. She had become known for her well-latticed apple pies after the commune tour's donation of apples and pear-apples. Now, her nimble fingers joined with Nora's. whose fingers were kept nimble by incessantly throwing dice in the Yahztee game. Her boredom had caused a slouch in her tall limber spine. "My husband," she remarked, "is now on crutches and would be honored to march as the crippled fife-blower in the Parade of the Fifes. He's already in costume, except for a black eye patch. Let's let him resemble an early-day wounded pirate instead of a modern day victim of an alcoholic binge. A red headache band would complete the ensemble."

"Ah, the big picture has a place for everyone. Even the kitchen staff donated a pair of white coats for the two English naturals. We'll use red dye and tuck in the sides, leaving tuxedo tails, and white grosgrain ribbon crossing their breasts—voile! Les and Roger become historical Redcoats in black boots and white long johns, supported by a thin black belt. A militia top hat improvised from poster board was lined with gold braid and sported a goose feather. It was molting time for the geese, so feathers were abundant around the walled-in chicken yard. The British Red Coats were out to steal the show.

Another natural was the swarthy skin Mexican-turned-Indian-scout. Manuel was back from escorting his Spanish-speaking colleague home. "Sure, count me in for a Navaho headband and some war paint." White arrows were painted on his face and bare chest. His black trousers exposed a knife handle near the right arm so the left hand could hold the flag staff.

Joey was a ragged soldier blowing a fife. "I performed in the Purple Fife Marching Band of New England," tooting a toy flute from the local store to prove his point. Having come from an oversized family, the oldest of seven, he'd left home to make elbow room. Finally overcoming dysentery, he looked pale and pounds thinner, but was able to toot what sounded like <u>Stars and Strips Forever</u>.

Allie joined the ladies with her stiffly starched yard of white cotton clipped from the ten yards she had purchased to take home. Having begged an ounce of starch to stiffen the material, she had painted an American flag. Once again, she was back in Dallas in an elementary art class. After applying the crayon colors of red, white, and blue, she melted the wax with the kitchen's hot iron. She still had a crayon fish on the wall at home to prove how permanent this process could be. Vivian was drafted to appliqué another square of cotton, sewing on an emblem of the United Nations flag. When completed, the five-petal star interconnected with red, white, and blue ending with a pointed star of white in the center. This star had '76 in its middle. "What a clever UN flag! "cried Allie, "only four years ago the General Assembly voted that Taiwan be replaced by a delegation from the People's Republic. Our hosts will be pleased with this flag, commemorating its thirty-year duration." She was glad she had supported Sandy's girl scouts who eagerly collected coins and sold cookies for UNESCO as part of the World Bank supporting health, food and agriculture.

While the ladies were engaged in parade planning, the men were constructing a launch pad. The fireworks had arrived. The first launch supported a rocket but not its destiny. "Zoom! Crash!" A window was not the intended target. How to apologize in Chinese? "Qing rang," suggested Allie. Better still, "mei yuan," U.S. dollars, as she rubbed her thumb and forefinger together.

The second launch pad proved adequate to launch rockets in the courtyard while the patriots marched for their slant-eyed audience. It was, at long last, July fourth, the Centennial Independence Day. Bravados joined the celebration by lighting firecrackers and throwing them just to show the U.S. and associates how Chinese live—on the edge. Americans flaunted their heritage, parading around the square with improvised flags and costumes. Drums and fifes had attracted an audience of well-wishers, laughing and cheering. The launch pad was the second invention, the first being Barney's ladder. The time to co-mingle was ripe. A wedding of cultures not seen since the overthrow of foreigners, the Boxer Revolt of 1900. But what was this rumbling at six a.m.? Had a real war been declared? Had she been mistaken about peaceful forbearance?

A quick flash in her mind of the Polaroid snapshot's background yellow, rendering her invisible, seemed now visibly flashing in the window, but why couldn't she move? What was holding her back, turning her into a blarney stone? She prayed for a way to flee, to become really invisible, not grounded to a spot half-way to the nearest closet where the yellow dress was hanging. She found her tongue and cried out above the deep roar, "B-Barney, a storm is coming!"

Only a moment before another window had crashed like the errant launcher on Independence Day. Intense ground lights spread a fiery rim, walls shifted, power lines fell. The telephone went dead. A powerful undertow was holding her hostage. When able to move she became aware of Barney shouting back over a louder roar. "It's a quake! Let's get downstairs! on the double!"

A crowded stairwell. Everyone moving very fast bumping into each other, excuse please, <u>dur' bu qi.'</u> The Guest House was pouring out people like a waterfall, a roaring waterfall! <u>Fie dee</u>! <u>fie dee</u>!, hurry, hurry! Mother Nature had declared a war, demanding her space, her quadrant.

No time was wasted in erecting tents. It was as if the Chinese had prepared for this. They were known to be expert at predicting earthquakes by well water levels, by eccentric actions of animals, growth rings of trees, ground tremors—ah-hah shaky legs in the dining room, she'd felt more than once, wasn't from an injury, nothing arthritic, but a warning! They had been unexpectedly moved to the second floor. The Chinese had obviously been expecting this for quite some time.

The first family-style tent was crowded and flimsy, but each had a canvas army cot to call his own. Barney had grabbed his short wave and was already tuning in to Hong Kong Radio. Luke, on the next cot had accessed Tokyo. "It sounds like deaths are countless and millions homeless."

Barney chimed in, "Shipping, mining, factories . . . all gone in Tangshan and Tientsin! He held up two fingers: two quakes, two epicenters!"

Oh my!" cried Leora, wringing her hands, "that is the very spot where the earth was divided into quadrants . . . foreign powers tried to take over the coastal region, then all of China."

"Tangshan, "added Allie, crouching closer to Leora, "held the life-blood of the country's economy, the most prolific anthracite coal mines in the world."

"The Seaman's Club in Tientsin is split in half." Jim and Nora hobbled inside the tent with another radio.

"Well, we won't be having lunch there again.," sighed Luke, "but thank goodness, supplies have been safely delivered to the plant for the last quarter!"

After a long pause of shocked silence, he jumped up. "What about our plant . . . how badly is it damaged, and how will it affect the contract? We're going out now to find out."

Allie and the other wives huddled together in their tent to wait for the bus to return their men . . . to find out everyone's future. In the meantime each would be escorted indoors only long enough to gather bare essentials for tent life. Their belongings would be moved to the first floor for easy access when the aftershocks subsided. Allie took a moment to look down on the domestic animals below. And what a sight! Roosters led the parade of feathered denizens lined up like well-disciplined soldiers marching to the open area where a gate had been blasted to the ground. Chickens, ducks, geese, no longer natural enemies, feeling aftershocks that people were not ever aware of, refugees bent on survival. The babble of honks, clucks, and gaggles was like a comic opera. She wished she knew their destination, their instinct, unknown to the human specie. Then she satisfied another curiosity: the guest house store on the damaged first floor. One glance confirmed rumors of the thrashing. Supplies were unceremoniously dumped on the floor and smashed, nature's fury unfurled as if some marauder had released his fury at the senseless regime. Allie was most grateful to have retrieved her sketching pad. Notes would be written behind sketches and not in the donated diary

Chapter 14

The men had nothing on the ladies when it came to latrine trips. They didn't do measurements or take away loose planks for souvenirs, but they had their cameras. A series of alcoves had no seats with only a couple of foot boards to stand on. The holes had been deeply excavated and disinfected. This was a bonus when compared to the average public privy! Allie prayed for future indoor privacy when the impish ladies began making a joke of their stances, using cameras to snap each other with their pants down. She couldn't believe the nerve of taking pornographic pictures without permission. When Nora approached the tent, Allie made her promise to give up the snapshot of herself in a squatting position, or at least tear it up when the roll was developed.

Who did she think she was? A paparazzo? The next offer to play Yatchee would be politely declined.

"How about offering her a hemlock cocktail?" What was Hans doing eavesdropping and causing her to blush. "Bong-bong" went the dinner bell, hanging from the roof rafter next to the dining room. The Yak bell was set up to be struck whenever food was ready to be served. All could occupy the hall for an already cooked meal, but only long enough to dine.

"After you, m'lady," grinned Hans, "we are being summoned to dine."

"Let's hope it's a cabbage roll and a pork chop today." She glanced at his sly grin.

"Aw, that's too special, I'll settle for Kung Pao stir-fries and Szechuan hot pepper sauce."

"I'll bet you a cocktail it's the daily dumpling, ping-tzu, made with kaoliang or millet flour. Horseradish may be a blessing. It goes with tou-tsai-fan, the millet gruel mixed with vegetables, what I call a substitute soup."

"Oh give me a home where buffalo roam . . . . just pass the noodles, peanuts, and sesame cookies . . . . uh oh, you are so right, he exclaimed as they approached the long table, "I see the offing; you can save the rice wine. Dumplings and soup on a buffet . . . good day, milady." Hans laughingly joined Roger, and Allie found Barney already seated after waiting for her to get in line.

The disrupted routine of dining, sleeping, and keeping cool was supposed to be off-set by a frequent flow of rice wine, a peace offering so to speak, but the devil would have his due. Lester became so inebriated that he jumped into a truck and drove it smack through the clothes line like a wild Viking. Later he inveigled tipsy

Luke into helping him move a refrigerator outside. With fingers on lips, he implied a secret invasion of the whole batch of stored wine. An unplugged fridge bulging with ole barley corn! What a feast!

More fruitless gestures—just to be patriotic while staggering on crutches, Jim supervised Joey's climbing the tent pole to add the United Nations flag to the already waving American flag. Joey was tall and thin as a reed, but his shaky climb caused onlookers to hold their breath "Be careful, ole boy!" hollered Roger, "Bamboo bends with the wind." He held down the limber pole with his weight, while others shouted, "Hang in there!"

Good humor turned into groans with the announcement of moving to another tent. By nightfall, the groans had reversed to joy when a sturdier pole was attached to a larger tent with sideboards and overhead lighting.

Tent life became less adventurous and more serious as occupants bonded in spirit. They shared and discussed books and magazines. They got better acquainted by venting their emotions, their true confessions of life back home. Liquor loosens the tongue—wasn't this from the book of Ecclesiastes? Leora tearfully whined, "My poor daughter's in jail for being a commie sympathizer. That's why we're here trying to figure out her beliefs."

"What does she think is so great about communism?" smirked Allie.

"She thinks everyone is equal or should be equal."

"Oh, she has a lot to learn. First, remind her that she was born in America. She has an obligation to her own country. Citizenship is a different type of empathy . . . an elementary text about China, Lewis' 1934 <u>Young Fu of the Upper Yangtze,</u> writes about naughty foreigners taught to steal from the rich as a form of ethics. Non-salaried soldiers were the main thieves. Desperate peasants rose to become cultural despoilers, thanks to Mao Zedong's seizing of power a few years later. Your daughter could even ponder a truth from Mao, "simple stirring leads to revolutions." He also says 'A revolution is not a dinner party.'" With that Allie left Leora to soak up her monologue. Then she sidled over to the sobering-up Limey sitting alone on a camp cot. Lester had gone on a rampage causing some debate between the Chinese. She recalled the watercolor valentine she had made at Les's request.

"Did your wife get the valentine you sent her?"

"Raa-ther, she loves it, but I don't think it's the only one she received. I . . . I bloody hate being gone so oft," he loosened the ascot around his scrawny neck, as if forced to tell tales out of school, "I grew up luckless . . . no class, so I haf' to work my ass off to make a quick shilling."

"Then I wish you luck . . . and the love of your Abu Ben Adam, awakening his peaceful soul if you remember that poem." She waved quote fingers in the air, and hurried back to her cot. The sketch pad was waiting if aftershocks would allow a steady hand . . . she would leave further English quotes to Roger who loved to recite from their classics.

She shook her shoulder to relax and turned on the radio for inspirational music then squeezed out colors on a palate. A news cast broke in with a more informative recast of the earthquake disaster as if to answer the very question she had been pondering . . ." roaring is caused by the primary wave that always occurs at the onset of an earthquake or rather a burst of P waves reaching the earth's surface. She splashed a burst of colors on her pinned-down square of silk, thinking aha! our benevolent hosts have been savvy to a precursor to recall one year earlier when 90,000 residents were evacuated from Haicheng two days before massive destruction-fore-shocks chartered for five years.

Allie had no precursor to rocks ignited like light bulbs stressed to the breaking point, no vision of broken windows, or the truck loads of wounded refugees being hauled to hospitals and clinics. Sitting in mud-smeared trucks with bloody headbands—fighting to survive, those in severe shock registered no pain. Face-saving numbers were not released or perhaps there were too many victims to count. No help needed, thank you, replied the fearful foreign take-over. Driving over a hundred miles for local help seemed desperate. Most of Hopei Province had become tent city, not only for homes, but open air hospitals . . . She could envision Bethune's Hospital over-packed with wounded, their bloody gauzes waiting to be replaced, their limbs needing first aid and acupuncture.

After the crews' first return from the plant construction, Barney made a fast leap out of the bus, "What the hell of a ride over bumpy rocks. Debris everywhere! Dangerous curves!"

"No wonder you were late. I hope the chefs are keeping our dinners warm." Her tone was soft and apologetic, and slightly uppity.

Roger, bounded out of the bus behind Barney, speaking with unusual excitement, "We just missed a landslide, but the boulder didn't have out names on it . . . what seemed offish were masses of tents leaning against skeleton-frames like miles and miles of. nesting aviaries, tent nests-cautious vultures! thinking another one is coming."

Luke took the platform to inform his passengers, as well as wives and gawking coolies of plant damage. "Fires have been extinguished and the tower is established. We will have to work overtime, but we will go home on time."

Hans would not be left out of the dialogue. "Cold showers, b-rr," shaking his torso, "the power is off; so beware of leftovers. I'm having junk food from cans and bottles." He growled in an

undertone, "Like the Bible says, 'Wine maketh the heart merry.'"
With a forefinger over his lips, in a hoarse whisper, "P.S . . . our
take-home privy boards have been name-plated."

What lewd souvenirs! How could he be so crude? She vowed to
burn Barney's memorabilia in the backyard brush pile.

Chapter 15

The men's tent was the noisiest with penny ante poker or bingo while the ladies read, wrote letters, or crocheted With lights out, the segregated expatriates had only hot August wind for lullabies and the flapping of canvas where guide ropes were loose.

Allie's cot was next to the open door flap making a staccato beat that caused long wide-awake hours, but finally droned her into a deep rem sleep. The popping sounds became the popping of ammunition. Thousands of ghosts at war with the Boxers, this time the coal mines were being exploited. She could hear her soap box cry, "Oh, please save the mines, the coal power for my little fan, my tent light and the lamps of China!" Her debate with the Boxers screamed of limited electricity-face-saving energy, of Tangshan's mines—richest in all of China: please save them, she prayed! White, skeleton Boxers argued that the mines were causing earthquakes. Their spirits would not rest in peace; their innocence had been sacrificed. What a strange dream! This is what she gets for having an overactive, subconscious, thanks to her minor in psychology with the world on her shoulders. She'd switch to another genre, blaming her ear-ringing for not having caught the entire data during daylight hours. Was the drum stick beating her for not responding to a "move it" demand, a <u>fie dee </u>or <u>ma shang, </u>or even I hate you, <u>aw tsung nay</u>! Crowds always reminded her of a wild west launch scene where everyone got caught up in the madness or a mob scene at Christ's crucifixion when her prayer for mercy was answered by a jump-forward rolling away of the grave stone or a cawing crow turned into a dove of peace. The strong arms of Barney and Hans belonged to Joseph of Armethia and Mary Magdalene, their love lifting Christ out of the tomb.

Bong! Bong! droned the bell. A megaphone substituted for the intercom. "<u>Joy geen,</u> good morning, preceded news and daily directives. A hot August day to be sure, destined to make changes.

A few hawthorns offered background shade. Not even a Chinese Tallow tree abounded like the one at home that gave her an allergy problem. Dreaming of Elm Tree shade with a cool glass of lemonade or a glass of ice tea proved fruitless as their oriental hosts believed that chilled drinks were unhealthy. Ripened cucumbers were being consumed by the passing parade, walking or cycling. Terraced tea groves no longer looked artistic, but chunks of surviving leaves were being harvested by children and grownups wearing back packs. Spasmodic waves of wheat fields were being sprayed.

Allie spent listless days studying rolled-up posters from her collection. Posters of orange trees in Shanghai showed workers literally buried in oranges. Wicker baskets overflowed from the harvesting picked by young ladies in white coats. Another poster had a long line of children marching for a medical check-up, barring their bottoms. Tiny soldiers already recruited—every ten or so fellows had a toy gun slung over his shoulder or in his belt. One came running with an adz, implying that he had been busy with carpentry. These were not the children performing at Peking's elementary school. A tug of war was going on in the political arena, children being innocent pawns. Right wing versus left wing.

The heat brought a dress style change, but only among the expatriate ladies. Out came flimsy vat-dyed garments purchased in Hong Kong. Leora and Nora settled for shifts—muumuus or sarongs. Allie gawked at them, astonished. When she found her tongue she apologized, "So sorry for starring but I can't get over how different you both look after almost a year in pant suits." She didn't add that their bulges were now exposed. She had never stopped wearing dresses exclusively. Her summer suit of pink pique would still be fine without the jacket.

Tent life finally reduced fifty percent, commensurate with receding of aftershocks. Dining, bathing, and eventually sleeping overnight in first floor beds became a daily directive.

The Bogaards planned their own ice cream farewell party before returning to Rotterdam. The successful sour kraut fermentation was from a home made recipe and so was the old-fashioned ice cream churning recipe. The ingredients were purchased during their R&R. Cranking the mixture made from cans of sweetened condensed milk, sugar, and vanilla took time and muscle. Young Joey began the crank, winding up with Barney, the most muscular.

After Joey's crank, he straightens up his tall frame, extracting his toy flute out of a side pocket and begins tooting "Yankee Doodle went to town ridin' on a poo-ny . . . arms locked to swing their partners for a make-shift square dance. Dutch lady Edda surprised everyone by announcing a line-up for the Virginia reel. "Choose your partner . . ." Joey tooted: buffalo gal won't you come out tonight and dance by the light of the moon.

It wasn't long until her moon-shaped eyes twinkled as she announced another line-up for home-made ice cream and began carefully unpacking salt brine and removing the rotary center. When she ran out of bowls, she quickly filled saucers, and tumblers with the fast-melting confection.

Roger contributed his last tin of English biscuits.

After feasting, someone's humming of Camp Town Races began a sing-song with A Bicycle Built for Two, In the Gloaming, White Cliffs of Dover. Memorabilia tormented faces so close to weeping. The Bogaards' daughter with hands on hips did a dainty heel-toe Dutch trip. Its simplicity being so contagious that others joined in, stomping out the social relief or the brief respite in the one-year journey. Not quite over for the Mueller's and Smiths still on contract.

Not intending to disturb his daughter's fun, Bogaards turned on the short wave for a Tokyo Radio recast of the earthquake's new developments. "Earthquake years are always the coldest. Manchurian winds are already whipping across the Great Wall. After shocks continue . . .

Chapter 16

On the ninth of September, while the village was still encamped in tents, a grim and very sudden order ushered everyone to a not-yet-disclosed function.

Allie was ready with her habitual camera in hand, but not for long. A Red Guard spotted her camera and looked very sternly at her. They were ascending the stone steps of a long vacated Buddhist Temple, but what was the occasion? Flowers everywhere. Roses galore, freshly cut stinging her nostrils. Then with a step higher, the bland odor of chrysanthemums permeated the crisp morning air. Such a crowd! Everyone in the village must be present. They were blocked on the marble steps with only a glimpse inside the vast cathedral with stands of pictures, more flowers. They could go no farther. Leora, elegantly garbed in black, elbowed her, then whispered in a drawl, "It's a memorial service for Mao. He passed away last night." Her camera was snatched, but she snatched it back and thrust it in her roomy handbag, remembering this to be a stunt she had seen Leora do. Empty store shelves were not to be snapped nor donkey carts unloading coal at the kitchen door. Mao's service would be the ultimate in face-saving.

Born Dec. 26, 1893-Sept. 9, 1976. Allie could envision the tomb of the poet and calligrapher, not the cremation he requested. Portraits were everywhere, though not as huge as that of Tiananmen Square positioned on the outer facade.

She could envision highway billboards springing up over night, showing Mao now flying in the clouds. Perhaps his claim of U.S. Imperialism would cease to be a real and present danger, or a paper tiger of self-interest. Perhaps tomorrow, <u>ming tian</u>!

Breaking up of the international family brought out the dairy-address books with future hopes and hints, "Iraqis treated us well, India is hot, hot. Go to South Korea."

Jobbers were given send-offs one by one. Officials directed the Guest House bus loading, waving <u>zai` jian`</u>, good bye, <u>bao zhong,</u> take care, or <u>guo` de kai xin</u>! Have a good day. Jim and Nora were the first to go with Jim's need to be hospitalized for leg surgery. Nora's medical family would see to his incarceration. Next came Mitch, a new father very much needed at a tornado damaged home to be repaired . . . He proudly passed around a snapshot that arrived in the nick of time, "My wife has a bouncing baby boy . . . but she's still recuperating from flying glass." Joey breathed a sigh of relief, as he hopped aboard. Color had returned to his cheeks. He grinned to think of his father's delight with the overseas pay check to help support that huge family of nine.

The British gave a "top of the morning" salute, gingerly leaping into the bus. The hosts saluted back with stern faces remembering the clothes line crash in the borrowed truck. The houseboy snickered to recall The Comedy of Errors hidden under Roger's mattress after a trip to Hong Kong. It had seemed like a fitting read for the life style of oriental entanglements. The book was confiscated but now it was nonchalantly returned with a handshake.

September 30th departure date found the Smiths well-packed, using the wooden box brought from home to hold excess household supplies. Not a coffin for a human body, so taunted the friends back home. It was their way of saying be careful!

Allie had been frantically painting to complete several items to be left behind. These she took to Hans who would be the last to leave. She wanted to make sure the Chinese kept them; if not, he would fall heir. They had given her a scroll with an eagle painted by Hsu Bei-hong reputed to be a famous artist. She would look up the hieroglyphics later—the title or message that always accompanied their art and usually spelled out peace, love, or honor.

The Smith send-off was accompanied by a startling line-up. It looked to be a block long. The complete staff of workers, not only officials, but kitchen staff turned out to wish them bon voyage The hospitality chairman who had asked them about drinking Molokai hopped on the bus to secretly thrust something in Allie's hand. She sensed his inappropriate behavior and dropped the object into a patch pocket of her grey tweed suit. She would examined it later . . . the look in his eyes expressed sorrow that she was leaving. The pride of acceptance was a great feeling to lift her spirits for a long time to come.

Beyond tent city the bus bounced over torn and dangerous roadways opting for smoother paving as they neared the Hopei capitol. Peking would be the first leap forward to home grounds. Barney noticed the spasmodic wheat harvesting. A vehicle seemed to be moving as fast as the bus. He waved to the six harvesters well equipped with lunch basket and bed rolls They waved back from the rear wagon of a tractor. "Hearts leaping high for the life-saving wheat." was that a poster heading or did I make it up?

Leaving a city of tents evoked a sense of gratitude for safe passage, carrying with it a lasting impression of haunted faces. Perhaps the faces longed to be trading places with the dreaded bourgeois. Did she sense some relief that a plant was built? or an opposite belief that it may have precipitated the quake. There was the never-to-be-forgotten scene of the animal march. If animals can cooperate, why not people? Those expatriates who thought they left their troubles at home knew now they'd come here to face them and go home repentant, with more grateful hearts. They could learn something from a Mao Saying: "it is necessary to interpret both facts and history of a problem in order to understand it; a mistake to see only good or bad." The coldest year on record was the way the radio described 1976 with Tangshan's earthquake causing 600,000 deaths, millions homeless and great economic damage.

When asked about living in tents, Barney assured the liaison office that it was no picnic, but the final tent was roomy and bordered by one-inch planks. "We flew a UN flag," added Allie. "I'll bet Betsy Ross couldn't have sewn faster than the duet of southern seamstresses."

The liaison secretary reminded Allie of the proposed shopping tour. An antique shop was in the offing, but Allie hugged herself and whined, "My warm trench coat is en route home. I thought the weather would let up."

"I have just the thing; it's an old coat but very warm." Whisking it off the wooden hanger and out of the closet, she wrapped the New York labeled pink tweed around Allie's shoulders. "Yours! It's an extra; you can keep it."

"Let's go!" she cried, a moment later, snuggling into her beaver-faux, "I'm still collecting dynasty costumes; they're a dime a dozen."

"Sure thing, I'll tag along. Our Japan Air flight isn't until tomorrow. Barney's doing some paper work."

Although antiques were sold as <u>Chinese,</u> some were suspected to be black-marketed Japanese or Manchurian. She snuggled in the well-insulated tweed, feeling good enough to purr like a cat, as the generous-hearted secretary settled for something later than Ming, perhaps Sung . . .

Allie found small items that would fit in her canvas tote bag. Thankfully, not all canvas was made into tents. Stone lions and vases were carved into miniature candle holders. A tightly crocheted pair of acrobats came in a domed-shape glass case barely small enough to fit her bag. The case was seamed together with crocheted-braid and lifted off the base. Thin, delicate eggury caught her eye with tiny canaries perched on plum blossoms, pandas chewing bamboo, Monarch butterflies sipping morning glory nectar. She had but to pick out a couple that looked securely glued.

Crocheted miniatures of dragons and griffins in their own display cases—someone had worked their fingers to the bone clicking the tiniest hooked needles available. Resurgence of oriental art was everywhere waiting to be redeemed. Origami, kite flying . . . and her gift! what was the pin awarded for? She fingered the metallic square that had a gold circle in its middle with a red flag, the emblem given her as a departure gift. A secret admirer, a gold ring, Chinese intrigue?

Mary Ranieri

She was finally getting homesick for a democratic life with peaceful dreams as she and Barney happily boarded the Japan Air wondering if the pilots were the tiger-pilot offspring they had dined with one year ago in the Peking dining room. A quick glance proved them to be too slant-eyed for half-breeds. In any event, they anticipated a smooth landing by way of Montreal, close to where her itinerant parents started from. And just perhaps they would kiss the U.S. soil like others have professed to do. Or at least wave kisses to a family-welcome with a toast of nothing stronger than a coca cola waiting for them.

About The Author

I am a potential MS from the University of Houston, my thesis having been postponded in lieu of foreign travel. Having studied under a scholarship and off campus creative writing, I published a book of poetry (Becoming all that I am) one year ago.

My one year in China during the reign of Mao Tse Tung was on a building contract, I decided to write about this span of time as an historical novel, using pseudoms for privacy.

Now a widow, I live a quiet rural life with six cats and nice neighbors.